Cracks through the Core

1951

Ladies of Bottlebrush Grove

Olwyn Harris

We have this hope
as an anchor for the soul,
firm and secure.
(Hebrews 6: 19)

ISBN   Softcover   978-1-923021-26-6
       eBook   978-1-923021-27-3

Published by: Reading Stones Publishing
Helen Brown & Wendy Wood
Woodwendy1982.wixsite.com/readingstones
Cover Design: Olwyn Harris Some of the cover elements were created using AI technology.

For more copies contact the publisher at:
Glenburnie
212 Glenburnie Road
ROB ROY NSW 2360
Mobile: 0422 577 663
Email: Readingstonespublishing@gmail.com

1. 1949

"Daisy, you don't have to settle for nursing when you have the capacity to be the surgeon. Did you even think about what I have said?"

"Yes, I have thought about it! I have no inkling to be dissecting people's bodies while they are anesthetised. I want to be *with* them. *Nurse* them!"

"Is this just because it is expected women are the nurses? What about being a doctor? You will end up feeling frustrated that you haven't given yourself the opportunity to work to your capacity. Your science subjects and maths are excellent now. You have passed all your exams."

"General Practitioner diagnose and prescribe. There is no real time for people. What can you achieve in a half hour consultation... or less?"

"I'm just saying you could do something much cleverer than wiping away old people's drool."

"Faith! I can't believe you said that! It sounds disgusting, until *that* someone is someone we know... someone we love. Then I would guarantee you would want a nurse who knows what they are doing; and doing it with skill and dignity and compassion. I believe you would consider it clever enough then!"

"I was so certain you would want to follow Philip to the hospital. You have always been great buddies. Why can't you be a doctor like him?"

"Because I am not him. I *am* going to the hospital where he works. He has inspired me in a different way. To nurse. Mum, tell Faith to give me a break."

"She is right Faith. If Daisy believes this is her calling... then what can I say? Would you have changed your mind if I had badgered you to do something other than teaching just because you had the capacity to do something different?"

"I'm not just talking *different*, I'm talking better." Faith frowned at her mother exasperated. "Ma'ma, Daisy is my very first graduate. She deserves more!"

Daisy stared at her in horror. "This is not about making you look good! Grief! This is *my* life! Surely all that study was about giving me options to do what I want. And I do appreciate what you put in, Faith, I really do. But I have deferred long enough and now it is time. I know I would not have had the marks to be accepted into this intake without your support. Faith, you have The Academy. Now it is my turn to have a dream!"

Faith burst into tears. Her mother quietly handed her a handkerchief. "Faith, darling... let her be. She has made up her mind."

"But she might as well become a nun. They will lock her away in those nursing quarters and we will never see her again!"

Daisy stood up disgusted. "Says you! When you left home it was years before you even set foot back inside our door. And if Gabe hadn't rescued you from the clutches of that stuffy city boyfriend of yours, you would still be there. I happen to love Lenwick, and I will come back. I promise you! But I have to go and do this first." Daisy put down her cup and turned around.

"I am going to pack," she said determinedly, as she left and closed the door to her room.

Faith rubbed her forehead and sighed. A wave of nausea hit her. She felt like she was losing Daisy. Her little sister had suddenly grown up. When did that happen? Her mother reached out and rubbed her forearm. "I know. I know. It never gets easier. It was like this when you left."

"Like this? Why didn't you say something! Oh Ma'ma, surely it was different! Did I really put you through this? And Philip?"

She nodded. "And Philip too. Probably worse with him. He is so busy it is hard for him to find the time to write."

"Oh Ma'ma. I'm so sorry. I had no idea. How could I ever do this?"

Salome nodded quietly. "You will be an amazing mother, Faith. Do not fear. You will."

Faith burst into another flood of tears. "But... but..."

"I know. Honey it is all right. This is the way our mother's heart gets captured by those entrusted to our care... whether we give birth to them, or they come our way by some other twist of providence."

"Oh Ma'ma, I know what you say is right... but try as I might, I can't get my head around it! I should be happy Daisy is so confident about the direct path she wants to pursue. Many people have no idea where they want to do and drift on for years. Why am I'm being so pig-headed about this?"

"Well, let me tell you what I notice. Your emotions are all over the shop. The things you normally take in your stride, have you baled up against the wall. You say you feel hungry and sick at the same time. And then you try and sleep it off, but you wake feeling that same exhaustion you went to be with, perhaps worse. But the hardest? I suspect the hardest of all, are the smells. That was when I always knew. There are smells out there I didn't even knew existed. Did you know lettuce leaves smell? I would have vowed such a thing was impossible until I was pregnant."

Her eyes flew wide open. "Pregnant? I am pregnant?"

"I would say so. Just a guess."

Faith did a quick calculation in her head, and gasped. "I am late. Very late. Do you think...?"

"I do."

Faith stared at her mother and then burst into tears again. "Daisy will never see her little niece or nephew. She's going to miss out on so much! I just thought I was rundown... ohh... this is terrible!"

"I'm pretty sure Gabe will think differently. I have heard you both talk about this. Are you sure there isn't some other reason you are so upset? I thought Gabe had agreed you would continue working while you could."

"Oh. The Academy..." A groan escaped her belly. "I was thinking about getting another teacher for when this might happen... but I hadn't seriously got very far. Now I have probably left it too late. I only have a few months to sort it out. I cannot close the school. I won't! Yet the reality is, if a teacher is any good, who in their right mind, would come to Lenwick to teach?"

"You did my dear. You did."

* * *

2.

Faith was too unwell to travel, so it was her husband, Gabe, who escorted Daisy to the hospital in the city. Daisy reported in and moved her boxes into the small room allocated to her at the nurses' quarters. The name plate on the plain timber door announced she had started on this extraordinary journey: *Nurse Galloway*. She stood on the steps to say goodbye to Gabe, awkward and uncertain. This was a long way from Bottlebrush Grove – the family farm where she grew up, barefoot and unfettered. It was a long way from Lenwick where everyone knew everyone's business. Suddenly Daisy felt very small. She gave Gabe a hug. "Tell Faith, she should believe in me. I will prove to her that this is what I am meant to do."

"You will do great. And don't worry about Faith. She will get used to the idea. She is so proud of you. All the family is. And here... you can keep an eye on Philip. It's about time someone could keep tabs on him."

When Daisy started her Preliminary Nursing Course, she absorbed the theory like a sponge. Foundational anatomy, body systems, disease pathology and nursing assessments did not intimidate her. She pedantically immersed herself in all the practical lessons of making beds, bathing, rolling bandages, shaking down thermometers, fluid-balance charts, blood-pressure cuffs, urinals and pan-rooms. She dived into her ward placements like a fish being released to swim in an enormous ocean. This was opening a door into endless possibilities. And although Daisy missed the quiet familiarity of Lenwick, the busyness of work was distracting and stimulating and challenging and inspiring. She could definitely make a difference here. She had no doubt.

Gabe was right: one of the best things about coming to this hospital was Philip. Her big brother was her childhood hero and her best friend growing up. She had missed him frantically when he left home to study at university, and Daisy had transferred all her affection for Philip into her books. If it had not been for Violet, her younger sister, she would have gone stark raving mad. And, of course, her little brothers managed to keep her grounded with their annoying pranks and their down-to-earth teasing. But now she was close to Philip again, and it made the city less like being in exile and more like an extension of home. When they got together for their weekly catchups, Daisy allowed herself one extravagance. She came armed with plenty of questions and forewent cheap hospital coffee for the indulgence of a thermos of rich, aromatic, brewed coffee for them both. As they sat together, ate toasted sandwiches with their coffee, Daisy interrogated him with the 'Whats', and the 'Hows', and the 'Whys' of all sorts of physiological and pathological subjects. Philip responded with methodical medical analysis, and she filtered and massaged his information so she could apply it from a nursing perspective. She didn't want to end up being feeling like the frustrated medic Faith's forewarning predicted. She believed wholeheartedly that Nursing was its own unique discipline... not a version of being a poor man's doctor.

All around her, experienced hard-bitten nurses told her, over and over, "Don't get personally involved." It was the mantra of the gold standard in professional nursing care. Yet Daisy was determined not to lose sight of the 'care' aspect of her work which had inspired her to start with. Personal is what made it human. Human is what motivated her to keep going despite aching legs and tired bones and watery hospital food. She had to do it this way, otherwise it would have been pointless to resist Faith's insistence on pursuing a more prestigious career. If her work was boiled down to organ systems lying on a bed, without a name, or a family, or a life, then nursing care was not care at all... it was a petri dish in a laboratory, like the place where Philip worked to pay his way through university.

Each nursing study block continued to challenge and fuel Daisy's interest in all matters of health and healing. When she was given her next ward placement, she was delighted. Children's ward. She really felt this would be a comfortable fit. She grew up around children. Her mother always had various foster kids in her care. But Daisy didn't count on what she encountered, as she stepped through those doors that first shift in the Children's Wing. The ward was crammed, even the corridors were full of constant distress that could not be alleviated. There was no time for story books. She ran from the moment she stepped inside the door, until the ward sister pushed her out at the door, at the end of the shift, with many extra hours piled on top.

As Daisy walked outside into the cold shadows after one late shift, she huddled under the tailored woollen cape around her shoulders. The irony that she wanted to nurse to have time for 'people' was a naive pipedream!

Fatigue hit her like the darkness of the night, as she walked back along the path to the nurses' quarters. She had done another double shift. There was no time for people here. The demands of the job made the patients incidental to all the tasks that needed to be attended to. This place was an avalanche of agony, and she learnt immediately there was a very specific culprit. Polio. Poliomyelitis. Infantile paralysis. Didn't matter what you called it... it was the same horror... over and over and over.

Parents came in hysterical; children were admitted screaming uncontrollably, gasping through the encroaching muscle weakness that lurked like a silent curse. It felt like those old-fashioned bedlam wards full of crazy people who had lost their minds. Only, in this case, their minds were fully aware of the horror they were faced with. Parents were escorted off the ward, leaving kids gasping and crying and panicked. Every shift, bodies of children who smothered in their own paralysis, were taken away. Every shift, children screamed at the callipers, and the braces, and the traction, all inflicted in an attempt to protect their muscles from the silent, creeping immobility that was coming over them. And then there was the Iron Lung section. Rows and rows of cylindrical tubes, heaving and hissing like a clutch of breathing dragons who partially devoured children, with only their little heads poking out of their jaws.

But even here, Daisy would not be deterred. Every shift she determinedly worked at being better able to manage the section that she was given. She dealt with the problems with increasing success, and soon the Ward Sisters would come to Daisy before their more senior student nurses. She became skilled at trouble shooting issues with the iron lungs, and she always tried to analyse the problem and sort a solution with the machines before the hospital maintenance engineer arrived.

One day, at the allocated visiting hour, one of the mothers came in with a small hard-covered book called '*The Red Book*' and offered it to Daisy to read. It was a most confronting thesis on an alternate therapy for Polio victims. It defied what was taught by Dr Telford – the resident specialist, in their lessons. As Daisy read through its pages, she was determined to find out more about this physical-therapy approach. There were a couple of things that Daisy kept coming back to. It was written by an Australian country woman, who had worked as a Bush Nurse. Daisy thought of Sister Blaine at home in Lenwick. She had the greatest respect for her, and felt she was of the same resilient ilk. Sister Blaine had continued to provide health care for the community after Dr Mortimer died, and she embodied the commitment and resourcefulness of working in remote Bush communities. And even though the author of this little red book – Sister Kenny, had no accreditation as a nurse officially, her experience with Sister Blaine gave her confidence that resourcefulness was a great teacher. The results Sister Kenny documented were a remarkable achievement, and the improved mobility of children after the acute fevers of Polio passed fired hope in many parents. Over and over, Sister Kenny presented the story of making a difference. The Americans embraced Sister Kenny's work like a celebrity and dedicated hospitals and rehabilitation centres to her name. But here in Australia, after decades of experience of working with children, even now, when she was retiring, her work was still shrouded in controversy. The medical world argued about where Kenny grew up; her unconventional use of heat, massage and exercise, and her scorn of immobilisation. She had a general lack of credibility because she didn't have an official piece of paper framed on her wall. It made not a scrap of difference that she co-authored *The Red Book* with a Doctor who *did* have the piece of paper. Daisy returned the loaned book with gratitude and went straight out and bought her own copy, along with its companion, *The Green Book*. Those books became her most used reference and she quietly started to work with some of the children whose mothers were advocates of Sister Kenny's work. Daisy could see improvement in the children and reviewed her own observations with Kenny's notes. It convinced Daisy of the validity of Kenny's interventions. But it was time consuming and difficult because there was a great deal of resistance to these techniques amongst the staff, and consistency between shifts was virtually non-existent. There were so many other things that needed attending to on the ward.

"Nurse Galloway, Sister Gilroy needs you in her office. Now. Nurse Evans will take over from you. Straight away please!"

Daisy frowned. She was rarely called into the Ward Sister's office. She scanned her patients in her mind, and quickly checked her note pad. There was nothing that she could identify that had been missed. She sighed and suspected that someone had again reported her use of physical therapies on the children. She had been cautioned a couple of times because she was stepping her toe over the line of accepted nursing duties. "Yes Sister. I'm going."

It was a long walk down the hall to the office, past the nurses' station. The corridor seemed to retreat into the distance like a tunnel. She wondered what the consequences of this reprimand would be. Would she be taken off this ward and sent somewhere else? Would they say it was to diversify her nursing education, but really was an action to remove her out of the way? Would she be suspended on a written reprimand; or denied a reference when she graduated? Perhaps, if it was serious, she would be denied the opportunity to graduate in the first instance? Daisy rubbed her forehead and tried to swallow her anxiety. Somehow, she had to stay. The need was so great, she absolutely had to stay. Daisy had already asked about the possibility of applying for a nursing specialisation on the Polio ward, but those opportunities were only available after she graduated. She knocked at the office door and a voice called her in. As she opened the door, she looked up surprised. Philip stood there in his doctor's coat. Sister Gilroy, stood stiffly behind the desk, and quickly came over to her. "Dr Frazer is here to see you. He says he is your brother."

Being related to medical doctor in a white coat obviously was an impressive skill for a second-year nurse. But Sister Gilroy and her admiration for her brother was forgotten as she looked into his serious eyes. "Hey Philip. What's going on?"

"Daisy Hope, you'd better sit down." He positioned a chair and pressed her shoulder gently as she cautiously sat. "I got a phone call from home..."

"From Mum? Oh. What's wrong? Is everyone okay? The baby? Is she okay?"

"Yes, Baby Lucia is fine. The boys are fine. It's Violet. She has a fever. She is critically ill. They think it is Polio."

"Violet? Oh no! How? But she is nearly sixteen. Surely she would be less at risk."

"Well, we both know, anyone, at any age, can catch it. And she has been a little delicate her whole life. How she contracted it is not important. Right now, we have to manage this. I'm going straight home and I want you to come with me. We need to bring her back here before she cannot be moved. Telford has collaborated the diagnosis and has agreed to treat her. This way she will access the best care. I have organised it with Matron, so we can leave straight away. I've borrowed a car; if we drive straight through it will be faster than the train, and we can have her back here and admitted quickly. This is her best chance."

* * *

3. 1951

"Nurse. I normally would just take a letter like this without comment. But I do have to ask: do you realise what you will be giving up once you submit this? There is no going back. Do you understand this?"

"Yes Matron, I do. But this is important. You can be assured I have not made this decision on a whim."

"But you finished your second year at the top of your intake. You are nearly there. Nothing could be so important that you would leave just before graduating."

"Something is more important just now Matron. My sister. She is not coping being here. I need to take her home."

"Ah yes. Violet Galloway, your sister. Dr Telford mentioned that you come back to the ward after your shift ends and put in many more hours looking after her. He also said you have a natural proclivity for nursing these long-term patients... and they respond well to your care. You do a lot of good, Nurse Galloway, so I need you to consider what is the best use of your skills: one person versus all these other patients that you help."

One person! This was not just some anonymous number in a file! Daisy swallowed her anger and spoke in a steady monotone. "Matron, I appreciate your concern. But Violet needs to go home, and I am the only one who can make that happen. I cannot put this off any longer. We will be going home as soon as I can organise her discharge with Dr Telford and Sister Gilroy."

"Then you wish for your resignation to stand? Don't you think that it would be more expedient to at least sit your third-year exams and graduate? Your sister will still get the care that she needs until then."

"Under normal circumstances I would advocate for that course of action. But these are not normal times we are faced with. Violet is fading away before my very eyes. I cannot delay this any longer. I need to take her home. I have spoken to my brother, and he agrees. This way she will have a nurse with her all the time. I will be sure that she gets the physical therapy that she needs. I have studied Sister Kenny's methods. I've read her Green Book and Red Book so many times I can just about recite it."

"Kenny is an outdated, dangerous, unaccredited renegade. She grew up in Warialda, of all places. She was schooled in Guyra... wherever that is. She is an uneducated imposter who has the audacity to call herself a Nursing *Sister*. Bush Nurse says it all. Just because she gets some doctor to rubber stamp her methods, doesn't make them valid. The Hospital board has made their decision based on the specialist recommendations to stay with less controversial treatments. You would do well, to keep your sister here, finish your training, and allow the doctors to do their job."

"I will not be moved from this. It is the right thing to do." Daisy looked up from the spot on the floor where she had focused her gaze. "But Matron... I wanted to ask if I could defer. Perhaps if all goes well, and when Violet is recovered... perhaps I could come back and make up my third year at a later time? I am committed to keeping up with my studies while I am home."

"That is certainly an optimistic request. But as I said before, I doubt that will ever become a possibility. The impact on your sister has been severe. I think you are not being realistic to consider that she will ever recover sufficiently for you to return to your studies any time soon. But since you were bold enough to ask, if you write a letter of application, and include a couple of references, I will submit it to the Nursing School Board on your behalf. The excellence in your grades, and your aptitude for study, will support your case. But Kenny will not serve your request, so please don't mention your unconventional sympathies. You would be wise to offer some conservative preference for the traditional nursing approaches of our facility. If the Board agrees, I will leave your position open for three years." The grim set of Matron's mouth indicated she didn't hold much hope that such a request would be supported and the commitment to hold her place open was a moot point. Nurse Galloway was throwing away her career.

"I am grateful Matron that you are willing to consider this. It is generous. Thank you."

Matron's eyes lingered on the closed door when it closed behind her. Yes, she was certain she would never see Nurse Galloway again. Shame. She had potential.

Daisy went outside and sat in the hospital gardens on a bench seat. Parents wheeled children in chairs along compacted gravel paths. She heard family members, in an alcove not far away, hoping for some space to privately cry, but no such privacy was available to them. Daisy reached into her pocket and pulled out a hanky. She shared their tears through the hedges. Her own heart was breaking too.

Violet, her beautiful Violet, was forever changed. The dream of nursing alongside her brother, had taken a very sharp turn. She would be nursing, but not in any of the ways she had pictured. If only she had not deferred starting her enrolment. If only she had studied seriously at school from the start and had not put it off, she would already be finished. But she hadn't. That was something she deeply regretted.

A heavy footfall on the gravel interrupted her thoughts. She looked up to see Philip standing there. "They said I'd find you here," he said as he sat down beside his sister, his face sober.

"I have spent a lot of time in this courtyard. It is a little oasis in an urban wilderness."

"Daisy Hope, you are doing a good thing... taking Violet back home. I really think she will do better there."

"I know... it has to be done."

"I came to tell you something else. I have received confirmation that my application to join the research team in Melbourne has been accepted." He had explored various options, even overseas. "The release of a polio vaccine is not far away! I know it! Violet missed out... but I want to make sure others don't have to go through this."

Daisy swallowed her tears. "You're doing a good thing too Philip. You haven't long finished your residency, and you are already putting your hand up. I'm going to miss you. This feels like saying goodbye to Dad all over again."

"I know. I know," he murmured. Philip eyes stayed solemn as they watched the parade of wheelchairs and callipers together. He was able to complete his medical training, even during the war, because medicine was a reserved occupation. He had received hate mail because he didn't enlist, even though some placements in the medical corps had been required. Now was his time for active service. "Dad's legacy was to actively engage in the fight — not to ignore it. That is what we are doing: following his example... both in our own way. This is war. It is hard. And it is costly. But it has to be done."

Her Dad had said exactly the same thing. Daisy's disappointment that she couldn't stay to finish her studies felt selfish. Here she was, bemoaning her own derailed ambitions, while Philip was enlisting. These children had problems that were insurmountable! She knew families cracked apart under the pressure of this disease. Well, she was not going to let that happen to her family. She pulled herself together, stood up and hugged her brother for a long time, before she went over to the nurses' quarters to pack up her things.

* * *

4.

Daisy answered the door.

"Who are you?"

"My name is Hugh Marcum. I am the schoolteacher. I have come to meet my new pupil, Violet Galloway... now that she is settled in."

"You assume that we are settled, Mr Marcum. We are still setting up the house to accommodate Violet's nursing needs. My brother-in-law is undertaking some significant renovations, including the porch. He had to installing a large sliding door so we could even get The Lung inside." The 'porch' Daisy spoke of was being converted to a large outside deck. Gabe's intention was that it would be large enough to support a daybed when Violet was well enough, should she want to go outside and see the sky. Violet missed looking at the sky.

"There are other things that need to be finished as well. I anticipate it will be quite a while yet before we are truly settled in. My older sister, Faith Trimboli, is the Schoolmistress of the local Academy. She lives next door with her family. So, we don't need a teacher and there is no need to extend yourself with pleasantries. I'm sorry you have wasted your time."

"I am aware of the geography of Lenwick, Sister Galloway."

"Since I have not attained accreditation of a Nursing Sister, you can call me *Nurse* Galloway." Daisy had long determined she was never going to be accused of the presumption of Kenny, who took on the title of Sister while she was unqualified.

"Humph. Very well, *Nurse*. Like I said, I have just come to introduce myself to Violet... as her *teacher*."

"Oh. Well, like I said, you need not have bothered. Violet is restricted to the Iron Lung. She cannot sit out for lessons. It is a shame that you are not like the rest of the town who treat us as lepers. Since they've temporarily closed the school from the epidemic, many people will not even walk past our gate. It would be convenient if you would just follow suit."

"Is she contagious? I understood she came home to rehabilitate."

"No, she is not contagious; she is well past the acute stages of the disease. But that hasn't stopped fear playing with people's ignorance."

"Well then, I think your observation adds weight to my request. Violet needs to meet people and get back into the routine of her lessons."

"She will be going back to the Flynn Galloway Academy when she is recovered. That Academy is named after my father. Our sister... as I mentioned... is the Headmistress there. My mother is chair of the Board. Since it is a family affair, Violet is already enrolled there. I apologise that your visit has been a waste."

"Hmm. Nepotism is my favourite form of partiality. Still, I don't see why you consider my visit a waste. I told you I came for a simple introduction."

Was the man thick? "It is a waste Mr Marcum, *because*, as I already stated, she will not be going to the public school. I'm sorry that you have bothered to come."

He seemed to relax. "Oh! I'm not from the public school. I work at the Academy. Your sister, Mrs Trimboli, is my boss."

She laughed. Mirthless and dry. "You work for Faith? That doesn't seem likely."

"I am pretty sure I would have a fair idea where I work and who employed me."

"But Faith would never employ a man. I know my sister."

"Well. I can't speak to her policy on equal opportunity employment, apart from her inclination towards family. But I can say, I have never had a fairer boss. I have been working here in Lenwick six months."

"What happened to Miss Mason? She was from out of town, the niece of the retired Methodist Church Minister. Faith put her on when I left for Nursing School. I can't believe you replaced her. Surely you are not serious!" Daisy stared at him like some sort of pathology specimen in a laboratory jar.

He raised his brow, and his serious eyes didn't blink. "I am completely serious. I am Miss Mason's replacement. However, what is the more pressing concern, is that you are forbidding me from meeting my student. Your mother requested I start working with Violet as soon as possible. You have already pointed out she is chair of the School Board. That means I am here under my employer's authority. I don't think you are in a position to prohibit such an introduction."

"My mother does not live here. And as Violet's nurse, I can prohibit whatever and whomever I like."

"Well then, can you please give me a time when your mother will be here, which would be a more suitable time for me to return?" He adjusted his tie and pulled at his jacket lapels.

"*Never* would be suitable. The day after tomorrow could possibly be an inadequate compromise. Like I said, we are still settling in."

"Okay. I'll come back then." He nodded briefly, turned on his heel, got in his car and drove away.

Daisy shook her head and went back inside. There were exercises to do.

* * *

"Oh. You're back."

"I hardly see how this could be a surprise to you. We agreed on the time when I would come back to introduce myself to Violet... as her teacher."

"You know, now is not a good time. I have just started her afternoon physical exercises. Come back tomorrow."

"Nurse Galloway, what is the problem? I just want to introduce myself to my pupil, with the view of starting some work. Your mother is concerned that she has missed a lot of school while she was away."

"Of course she missed school. Every minute of it! But that is not the greatest priority just now."

"Don't you think this is something her mother would determine?"

"Oh my goodness, you are persistent! Okay. Two minutes."

"Thank you." He stepped inside the little hallway.

"Wait here. Give me a moment to prepare her... she needs to know that you are coming in. She is shy."

"Shy?"

"Yes. Shy. It means she is nervous around people she is not familiar with."

"Which is why I am here."

"Wait, then." Daisy disappeared and then returned with a nod. "In here."

Hugh followed her into the living-room. The Iron Lung dominated the room. He could only see his pupil's head poking out the end, as if she had been swallowed by a giant, iron monster that hissed and heaved. Daisy pointed to where he was to stand so that he could be seen in the mirror hanging from the top of the Iron Lung. Violet's eyes were shrouded in embarrassment, and she turned her face away. "Good afternoon Violet. My name is Mr Marcum. I was asked by your mother to come and introduce myself. I am the teacher at the school... at your sister's Academy."

"Humph," she grunted to the wall.

"I know you have a demanding routine, but I would like to call on you again tomorrow."

Violet glanced at Daisy, and then looked back at him...doubtful, but she shrugged and rolled her eyes and nodded.

"Great. I will see you tomorrow. Perhaps then we could talk about the school subjects you like." He nodded to Daisy as he went to leave. He put up his hand. "No bother. I'll see myself out. I know you are busy."

He returned the next day, at exactly the same time. Daisy stood sentry, stern and severe, close by. Violet looked at him in the mirror. "Good afternoon Violet. I am Mr Marcum. I came yesterday. Did you remember that I would be here today?"

She nodded faintly.

"I said yesterday that we would talk about which are your favourite subjects. Did you think about that?"

She shrugged.

"Well, I have an idea. I will mention some school subjects and you can tell me... one to ten, how much you enjoy those subjects. Ten means you love them passionately. One means you would rather go to the dentist."

Violet raised her brow and smiled faintly.

"Maths. One to ten. How much do you like Maths?"

"Two."

"Okay – that tells me you are not a fan of mathematical problems. What about science?"

"Three."

"See... I already have some information. Science is preferred to Maths. But still not enthusiastic. You are doing really well with this. Reading?"

"Four."

"Oh well... here we have progress. Reading is winning the race at the moment. What about writing essays?"

"One. Don't mind it, but I can't do it now... obviously."

"Hmm. Well. As I am a teacher, I am going to give you some homework. Since Reading won the race, I want you to think of four different types of things you like to read. It might be pretend stories; or newspapers, or information on a particular project... like caring for animals, or cars, or cooking food. Or perhaps stories about real people. I am going to see if we can problem-solve a couple of things to make the process of reading easier for you. I would like you to help us with these ideas so we can find something that will work for you. Remember, I want you to tell me four things you like to read, and I will be back tomorrow. Good afternoon, Violet," he said with a smile.

Daisy walked him to the door. "You do realise Violet is sixteen years old. You don't have to speak to her as a child. Please, at least give her that dignity."

Mr Marcum looked shocked by her rebuke. He nodded and paused before he left. "I will try and do better."

* * *

With the predictability of a clock Mr Marcum returned. Rather than standing in the middle of the room, this time he pulled a chair over. "Is it okay if I sit? It will make talking with you easier." She nodded. "Do I need to adjust the mirror?" Adjustments were made. "So how did you go with your homework? Did you think about what you like to read?"

Violet nodded.

"Excellent. I asked for four things. What is at the top of the list? What is your favourite reading material?"

"Magazines. But we don't get many out here in Lenwick." She spoke between the hiss-whoosh of the lung machine.

"Which type of magazines do you like. Farming journals, or scientific publications?"

She smiled and shook her head. "Fashion magazines. I like those."

"Fashion? Well. I see your eyes light up when you mention that. That is obviously something you enjoy."

"I wanted to work with Miss Townsend... to learn dressmaking... but I never will now... obviously. She had polio too. One of her legs is thinner than the other... and one of her shoes are blocked up."

"Well, I am a fan of the saying, 'Never say never'. What is the second thing you like to read?"

"Umm... nothing really. Stories perhaps."

"Would that be adventure, or romance, or science fiction? Or something altogether different... like chilling horror stories?"

"Mother would never allow that! Mystery. I liked the puzzle... of working out the clues. But I was never a bookworm like Daisy."

He raised his brow and glanced at Daisy standing stiffly by the door. "Bookworm? Well... I didn't pick that. Mystery, you say. Your third preference?"

"Newspapers, I guess."

"Newspapers. The advertisements... or the political commentary... or the 'lost-and-found' section?"

"I don't think you will approve."

"I don't have to have the same preferences as you, just as you would not have the same preferences as me. What we enjoy reading is personal... unique as the lovely colour of your hair."

Violet blushed. "Well... the social section. I like to know what people are doing."

"Oh. Some call that the 'Gossip Column'... but I like to think of it as a way of connecting with our community, feeling that we are part of what is going on around here. Would you agree with that?"

"Yes," said Violet, looking at him curiously. "That is it exactly."

"And number four. What did you identify as your final preference?"

"Might seem strange... but recipes. I miss cooking. I used to do it a lot."

"Hmm. That would be a big change for you, I can see that."

She nodded.

"Well Miss Violet Galloway, I can tell you are a diligent student. You have done very well with the homework that I set for you. Now for tomorrow's homework. I would like you to look through a newspaper. I even brought one with me, and hopefully your sister can help you. I want you to find three people or events that are familiar to you, or that you find interesting. We can talk about them when I return. Just three things. Okay? Any questions?"

Violet shook her head.

He stood up. "Very well. I will see you tomorrow." He walked past Daisy standing by the sideboard that had been adapted as a washstand and held a pile of dressing trays. It made the room less like a loungeroom and more like a hospital ward. "Nurse Galloway. Good afternoon." He paused and came back to where she stood. "Tomorrow when I come back, could I have a moment of your time? There are a couple of things I would like your opinion on. I think it would be best to discuss them privately."

"Hmm. I guess," she said, with a frown.

"I won't take up too much of your time. Tomorrow, then."

* * *

Hugh spoke softly in the hallway. "There was a specific purpose when I asked to talk with you yesterday. I want to know if you had come across some sort of bracket that could be set up to hold books while Violet is in The Lung?"

"I remember one father set up a contraption for his son. But it was dismantled because it was large and clumsy and got in the way in the crowded ward. Besides, we didn't have the time to turn the pages for him anyway."

"This means our design needs to be compact and preferably managed independently. I was convinced that this was a problem that would have already been addressed."

"Well, it may have been... but like I said, we did not have the space, nor the time monitor such things on the ward. As far as I know there is no standard device like you describe."

"Well, Gabe and I have talked about it. I was thinking of some sort of book stand or clipboard like this." He took out a note pad and leafed through some rough sketches and showed her.

"Hmm. Well, if it did something to alleviate her boredom, then that would be worthwhile."

"Which of these ideas do you think would work best? You are the one who knows Violet, and you will have to work around it."

Daisy shrugged and the turned the pages. She pointed to the most basic configuration.

"Thank you. That has been helpful." That was all he said as he stowed his notebook. Then he nodded and left. Daisy stared at his back with a frown.

Gabe delivered his prototype which was something like a tripod with a stand that held a clipboard. He made a rudimentary mouth device which was a rubber thimblette over the end of a stick, that they hoped would provide Violet a way to turn pages by herself.

When they showed the gadget to Violet, Daisy looked at the setup sceptically. "I doubt these will work," she said with a frown. Violet refused to give it a go, so they left it there in the hope she would try later.

Before Hugh left, he stopped on the step and shook his head. "I appreciate the idea needs some work, but if Violet is going to be on board and help us refine it, she needs to know you support the idea. Whenever she catches a whiff of your disapproval, she shuts down. I've seen it. You are making this harder for her than it needs to be."

"I see no point in getting her used to doing homework in The Lung when the whole goal here is to get her out and live normally."

"And that is a worthy ambition. One which I support wholeheartedly. This is not to inhibit her progress, but to support her work towards it. Even if she is only in there for another fortnight, I am here to try and make tomorrow's learning smoother for her."

Daisy looked at him steadily. "I do not like you Mr Marcum."

"Well, without seeming presumptuous, I have already gathered as much. Your disclosure is not a surprise. Although I do admit, I have no idea why, so any light you can shed on that matter would be appreciated. Mrs Trimboli trusts me enough to employ me at her school... even in the face of some very specific gender bias... which, as you clearly pointed out, is not in my favour. Your mother trusts me enough to insist I tutor Violet, even when other parents are too terrified to either let their kids outside, or outsiders inside. Your brother-in-law was more than willing to help manufacture this gadget. I do not understand what I have done to offend you so seriously in such a short time."

"You know, I don't actually have to explain myself to you."

"True. But how can I make something right... when you won't even discuss what has gone wrong?"

"This is not about me, or you. This is only about what Violet needs."

"Finally! We have found some common ground. However, if there is something I have done, I will try all in my power to fix it. But in the meantime, can we please make a pact to work together to help Violet get back on her feet, back to doing life?"

She narrowed her eyes. Why would he make his interference sound so altruistic? Mr Marcum... playing the role of Tarzan, sweeping in to rescue Jane. Well, whatever he did would not change anything. It was Daisy who slept with one eye open, and her ear attuned to the whooshing rhythms of that blasted Lung. "Mr Marcum... if you think for a moment that I came home to do anything less, you are very much mistaken. I suppose you will visit again tomorrow. But in the meantime, you will have to excuse me... my work is less flexible. I cannot clock-off like you do. I have things I need to get ready for tonight. Good evening." She closed the door behind her. He heard the lock turn.

* * *

5.

Mr Marcum grinned. "You are pushing me, Violet. I asked for three things... and yet you have done extra. Perhaps I should have set higher targets. I think your mother will be very pleased. Now for your next project. Your sister Faith has lent me a recipe book... and I want you to choose something that you would like me to cook for you."

"You are going to cook? That's a bit weird. Men don't usually like cooking."

"Actually, some of the world's greatest chefs are men. But you are right, I personally don't like cooking at all. And I am terrible at it. But the point of a recipe is that if it describes the steps well, anyone should be able to achieve a standard outcome. I need you to choose something that is explained well and simply. If it is not clear, you might need to add additional explanations to help me. But there is a catch. Make sure it is something you are willing to eat. Regardless how it turns out, you must sample it. Do we have a deal?"

She nodded and her eyes smiled. "What if I choose something tricky?"

"Well, like I said, the obligation is that you are willing to taste it. So choose carefully, or we'll be suffering through a disgusting afternoon tea together. You said you liked reading recipes... so I encourage you read carefully and choose with discernment."

He walked out, and Daisy followed him to the front gate with a frown on her brow. "If you think this is a way to get Violet to eat, I'm sure your amateurish attempts will fail. Both my mother and Faith are excellent cooks, and yet Violet refuses almost everything they make to tempt her appetite. Swallowing in The Lung is difficult. She has to find the rhythm of it... between the pressure cycles."

"That sounds like the most uncomfortable ordeal. And I did not lie. I am a terrible cook... but my intent is not about getting her to eat. I want to find ways to give Violet more power in her very powerless life. Even if she eats half a mouthful of a biscuit, it will be a biscuit that she has chosen, and that is progress your mother has suggested she will be happy with."

"Are you criticising the way I am managing Violet's diet?"

"Not at all! You have your areas of expertise, Nurse Galloway, and I have mine. Even you acknowledge that as her teacher, I am afforded a little more flexibility than your own particular routines. My first goal is to get her reading again... however trifling, or frivolous it might be judged by others. Reading has to have a purpose. Why not read a recipe and test the teacher's inept culinary skills? That is a challenge I would have enjoyed as a student. I think it sounds like fun."

Daisy frowned. "Fun? I think you are taking liberties with your role."

"I would rather think of it as using creative license... or initiative. Violet's circumstances are restrictive beyond what I can possibly imagine. To engage a student's learning under these conditions is a challenge I have never encountered before. I have no agenda Nurse Galloway, other than Violet's wellbeing. I assure you."

"Humph." She sounded unconvinced.

Violet chose an Upside-down Pineapple Cake. He stared at the photo in the recipe book with his mouth fixed sideways in a thoughtful twist. His frown disguised his amusement. "Violet, I was hoping for some leniency. Did you consider my inexperience in the kitchen? I was expecting cinnamon toast, fairy bread or chocolate crackles."

"You said it was my choice. I have read the method. It is not hard."

"Perhaps for someone with experience perhaps. Look at that picture! I think it is very unlikely I could cook anything that would turn out looking like that. This is going to be a disaster. Did you remember that part of this assignment was that you committed to eating this?"

"You have admitted defeat even before you have started."

"For good reason. I would not have you survive polio, to end up dying from my cooking!"

Violet grinned. If it had not been from the pressure constricting her lungs, it is possible she may have even laughed out loud. "I have an idea that might help," she said.

"You do? Oh, I hope this is good, because I am going to need all the help I can get."

"Cook it here in our kitchen. I can talk you through the steps. You can ask questions and Daisy can help too."

Daisy looked up from where she was sitting reading her nursing books. "Oh, my giddy aunt. I am not going to rescue you from your own floundering life-raft when you set it adrift yourself."

His frown deepened. "Poetic. But I think Violet has identified a very realistic solution."

"No! I do not have time to muck around in the kitchen just to make you look good," insisted Daisy.

Hugh glanced between the two sisters. "Nurse Galloway, what do you need for Violet's very good idea to be put into action? I will owe you. You can ask any favour of me in return."

"You may think I am poetic, but you are pathetic. I don't need favours from you."

He stood up straight and squared his shoulders. "Very well. I will leave you out of this *mix*. But I will *stir* myself to ask permission to use your kitchen. In a *pinch*, Violet can *weigh* in and step me through the recipe. I really can't *beat* her very sensible idea."

Violet rolled her eyes and chuckled, but Daisy was unmoved by his attempt to be witty. "No, this is not a good idea. The oven is unreliable."

Hugh shrugged. "Gabe told me you were a tough crowd. And he also mentioned he upgraded the oven."

"He did, yes, before we came home, he redid the whole kitchen. But it is still does not cook evenly. The combustion-stove that Mum replaced years ago, was better... and it was not great either."

"It must work satisfactorily, enough for you to use."

"Barely. Our meals are cooked by either Mum or Faith. I really only use it to sterilize instruments." She tilted her head. "Okay. I won't prohibit you from making a fool of yourself Mr Marcum. Go ahead."

"Are you willing to do this on Friday? Great! I will cook afternoon tea here in your kitchen as Violet suggested. Violet, we have identified another dimension to this challenge: there is an unreliable oven to work with."

"Sure," Violet said. She blinked and shook her head. "A cooking disaster is not the worst thing that has happened in my life," she said philosophically.

He laughed and winked. "Are you familiar with food poisoning or cakes that flop?"

Violet shook her head. "I meant Polio."

"Oh. Well, I can't argue with that... definitely worse. I'll bring the ingredients on Friday, and you will tutor me in whipping up a Pineapple Upside-down Cake."

* * *

Hugh rocked up with a stiff brown paper bag filled with groceries. He piled the flour, brown sugar, butter and tinned pineapple, with a jar of glace cherries, on the kitchen table. He reported to Violet for duty. He propped up the open recipe on her bookstand, and they went through the ingredients he had brought, and the method together. "You will have to go next door, and borrow a cake tin from Faith," Violet instructed.

"Oh? I assumed a cake tin would be basic kitchen equipment. And I was not counting on publishing my attempt at this endeavour to the whole neighbourhood."

"We need a cake tin to bake a cake."

"True. What size? Big or small."

"Nine-inch round."

"This is data I can work with. Back in a tick."

He knocked at her door. "Hugh," Faith looked at him curiously. "Gabe is not home."

"Well Boss," he said seriously. "Violet has sent me over to borrow a nine-inch round cake tin. We are baking a pineapple upside-down cake."

"Violet has you baking... a cake?"

"The deal was that I would try this... if she taste-tested it. It should be noted that I have had no success in cooking to date, so this is a rather ambitious project. But she is willing to give it a try, even at the risk that she will never want to eat again."

"Your lack of cooking abilities has had the whole community supplying you with a lifetime of casseroles, even while you are at the boarding house." She shook her head with a grin. "It would be ironic if Violet can accomplish what a whole generation of grandmothers has been quite unable to achieve since you arrived."

"That is yet to be determined. Just now, I need the said cake tin. Please?"

"Sure." She grinned as she handed it over. "I may add Home Economics to your subject list."

He laughed. "At your students' peril, I fear. How about you wait to see whether I even survive this session in Daisy's kitchen?"

"I'm surprised Daisy agreed to this."

He shrugged. "She decided not to interfere. She is reserved, and like Pilate, she has washed her hands of this pending disaster. Probably wise."

"Daisy doesn't like you, does she?"

"That is harsh. I would say that she hasn't made up her mind yet."

Faith flicked her wrist for him to get going. "I know Daisy. I would say she is quite certain."

Hugh presented the cake tin to Violet, and she have him instructions on how to grease it. Then she stepped him through how to make the melted butter and brown-sugar syrup coating on the bottom of the pan... arranging the pineapple pieces and the decorative cherries. While talking to Violet about measurements, fractions and additions, he sat creaming butter and sugar. The discussion became an extended Maths lesson because Violet insisted that his creaming needed to be smoother, and he sat beside her with a wooden spoon and kept beating. When she finally approved, he went out to the kitchen to mix up the batter but dropped an egg on the floor. Hugh provided a running commentary from the next room on his attempts to scoop up the slippery goop. The next egg cracking attempt shattered fragments of eggshell through the mixture, which had to be fished out. Then the flour and pineapple juice were added... and stirred through. All of this had Violet grinning. Finally, the cake batter was poured over the pineapple pieces. By the time Hugh slid the pan into the oven, he looked like he had been in a food fight... and lost. There were streaks of flour through his hair, batter over his shirt, syrup up his sleeve.

When he came back in to report that the timer was set, Daisy looked up from her study book. She didn't even crack a flicker of a smile. "That simply means you have twenty minutes to make sure my kitchen is as pristine as any nurses' dressing-room. I wonder how you convinced Faith you can teach science and yet my kitchen looks like a grocery shop exploded? Your science lessons must be a disaster."

"I will have you know I run a very tight science lab."

She shook her head baffled. "Make sure it is clean," she said firmly.

He grinned at Violet and winked. "I think this means that the school bell has rung for recess. Why don't you run out and play, and I will go and sort the kitchen so we can share a cup of tea and cake before I leave. Afternoon tea is twenty minutes away."

Violet laughed and shook her head... and Hugh went into the kitchen to begin wiping benches and do the washing up. He was running the water into the sink when he heard Daisy hiss behind him. "You are a tactless, thoughtless, inconsiderate, insensitive brute! How can you joke about this?"

"I'm sorry. I would say that this kitchen is evidence I am taking this very seriously. I have never tackled any domestic project like this. I said I will clean it up... and I will. Your benches will be returned to their disinfected hospital pan-room state before our cake is cooked."

"This is not a joke!"

He went to say something and then paused; he looked past her to the open door. Very carefully he put the bowl in his hand in the sink, wiped his hands and went and closed the door. "Violet does not need to hear Mummy and Daddy squabbling," he said quietly and evenly. "I know you are under a lot of pressure. I will clean it up and then we will sample our experiment." He looked at the timer. "Ten minutes left to cook... so with cooling time, a quick cuppa and a taste-test, in forty-five minutes, an hour at the most, I am out of your hair. And then your hospital ward will return to its morbid, silent, sterile state. Hang in there, Daisy Galloway. I am confident you can do this."

He turned and started washing the dishes. Daisy stared at his back. "Don't you dare hurt Violet, or I will personally see that you leave this town without a reference and never return!" she said with emphasis before she firmly opened the door and left.

Hugh said nothing, but continued to wash the utensils, and saucepan and measuring cups. He wiped the bench and dried up. He was on his way to issue Violet with homework, when he heard a clatter at the front door. He raised his brow, as Jimmy and Joe bundled into the room.

"Hey Sis," said Jimmy without ceremony. "When are you going to stop lazing around and get up and do something?"

Joe jumped up onto the top of the Iron Lung, stretched out full along the top of it, staring down at Violet over the edge, pulling strange faces at her around the mirror that was positioned there to help her see about the room.

"Creep," he said.

"Right back at you Creep," she said without blinking.

"Good afternoon gentlemen," said Hugh seriously, as he walked back in.

"Hi Sir," Jimmy said, poking around the various things Daisy had laid out on the sideboard.

"Boys! What have I told you? First thing... go and wash your hands. Now!" Daisy stood at the door with her hands on her hips. "Use soap!"

"We were about to have some afternoon tea. Would you like to join us?" called out Hugh as they obediently left for the bathroom.

"Sure," said Jimmy. "What have you got? Smells good."

"Upside-down pineapple cake."

"No way! Daisy did cooking? Nice!"

"Well no. That is the catch. I made it, and it is yet to be determined whether it is edible."

"You? Why did you cook?"

"It was part of Violet's lesson."

"How is cooking a lesson, if you did all the work?"

"It is about communicating, explaining and describing. And I might add, she did well. At least, I think she did. But like I said, we are yet to taste it. You both can mark this assignment – an accumulative score," he said with a grin. He checked his watch. It was time to take it out of the oven, and he went to do that.

"You have to let it sit and cool, before you turn it out," Violet reminded.

"Okay. Well, let's play a game of Euchre while we wait. Boys, are you in?" he said as he pulled a pack of cards from his bag and started dealing them. "What about you Daisy... will I deal you in too?"

"You already have four players. I have to study." She picked up her book and took it into the kitchen. But she positioned her chair facing the door and watched their antics while she reread her chapter on respiratory diseases.

Hugh refocused on those around him and turned over a card. "Spades are trumps. Let's go. Violet this is your hand... just point to the card you are going to play." He lined the cards up on her book stand and adjusted the mirror so she could see the play on the small table beside them.

When afternoon tea was served, the boys good-naturedly decided that adding eggshell to the recipe created too much crunch, and Violet had failed her assignment. With full mouths, they demanded that she resubmit the assessment so they could mark it again next time they visited.

* * *

6

"Close your eyes Violet, I have a surprise. Are they closed?" her teacher said mysteriously.

She nodded.

"Okay. Don't peek. Not until I'm ready. Okay. Now."

She opened her eyes. And gasped. There on her book stand was a magazine. Colourful and bold. The glitz and pizzazz of a fashion house had walked into her room.

"Oh Mr Marcum! This is wonderful. Where did you get it?"

Daisy heard the excitement in her voice and came in and stood at the door, watching.

"There is a subscription in the name of Violet Galloway at the Newsagency. This is the first of many issues to come," he said.

"A whole *subscription?* Really? How?"

"As a student you don't have to concern yourself with 'How'. Your concern is what you do with it now."

"Oh! This is my favourite thing to read in the whole world."

"Beautiful. Well, you do that... and report to me tomorrow four things that this glossy little publication has been able to offer you. Four things – and I want two clear reasons for choosing each of them. Make them big." He picked up his bag. "I will see you tomorrow."

Daisy followed him to the door. "Thank you for doing that."

He shrugged. "It is just a subscription."

"No, I meant her voice... it sounded like the Violet I grew up with. It reminded me of the last Christmas we had at home before Dad left for the war. I haven't heard that in a long time."

"Daisy, you have to deal with difficult, and painful routines. And because you do that well, Violet is so improved. She told me she is sitting outside The Lung for longer periods each day, and she is getting better at... she called it 'frog-breathing', whatever that is. When she first came back here, I was told that she would never be outside that machine, at all. Yet she is getting stronger. That is completely attributed to your care Daisy. I have the privilege of being able to connect into that strength and identify some things that might bring back her sparkle. She told me when we first met, that fashion is her passion. Plugging into passion is easy because they want to pursue it."

"You paid for that, didn't you? I know Faith wouldn't have the budget for something like that."

"Like you said, hearing that tone in her voice... that is reward enough for ten subscriptions."

"Well, I'm sure Mayor Saxton at the Newsagency will be pleased enough for the business. Did you know his family's name was Sultzer before the war?"

"Lots of German names disappeared then. I didn't realise he was the Mayor though. He gave me a discount when he found out it was for Violet... as part of his community contribution. I am just pleased it is motivating my student to read. Thank you, Nurse Galloway. I know it adds to your work, setting up her homework and turning the pages. I don't take that for granted."

"She does pretty well with the mouth-thingie you made. We are on modification 3.8."

"Gabe made it. Thank you for encouraging her."

"You are not too keen on taking credit, are you Mr Marcum?"

"Only where credit is due. I am one small cog in a very large-hearted community. That is the reality of being here. I must go – there are other students to visit before it is too late." He nodded and paused as he turned to go. "Thank you, Nurse Galloway."

"You thank me? What for?"

"For giving me space to be Violet's teacher. *That* is my passion."

* * *

"Violet, I have brought a visitor with me today. We've talked about how to interview a community member. And you have interviewed Gabe, and your mother as a member of the school board. Now I would like you to interview someone whom you don't know well. Remember the questions you asked the others? Well, this is a good place to start, but when you are listening, if other questions come to mind, then don't be afraid to ask those too. This person is very busy, so it is very generous of her to give up her time. You have twenty minutes."

"How am I going to talk to someone I don't know for twenty minutes?"

"The point of an interview, Violet, is that you ask questions so that they do the talking. Just like we practiced... okay? Are you ready?" He went out to the hall and ushered in the visitor.

"Oh. Miss Townsend! Good afternoon." In Violet's eyes, this woman had celebrity status. She made clothes. She had also contracted polio and was still standing.

Miss Townsend walked into the room with a limp. One of her shoes was built up on the sole, and it made an uneven clunking sound on the floorboards. The smell of camphor necklace she wore was pungent. "Good afternoon Violet. Mr Marcum asked me to come and talk with you. He said it would help with your assignment."

"Thank you, Miss Townsend."

She sat down stiff, staring awkwardly out the window, not able to look at Violet's head poking out the top of the machine.

Violet asked her first question. Miss Townsend did not respond.

Mr Marcum sat in his usual place by Violet and cleared his throat. "Hmm. It seems Miss Townsend is not hearing you because the The Lung is noisy. Would it be okay with you Violet, if I repeat your questions? My voice is louder."

She nodded, relieved.

"Miss Townsend, Violet has asked how you initially became interested in dressmaking?"

"Oh, of course. Well..." and although she started tentatively, she had a captive audience, and it didn't take long before she launched into her family story. Her mother was a tailoress, and the haberdashery shop was originally opened by her mother when they moved here during World War One. But her mother's specialty was formal suits, for both men and women. Miss Townsend loved colourful fabrics as a young person but was never encouraged to use them. When she took over the shop after her mother passed, she experimented with different fabrics and how this changed the whole look and feel of the garment. "I thought some of them were quite pretty," she said rather self-consciously.

Mr Marcum relayed the first couple of questions, but soon Miss Townsend was talking freely. Twenty minutes had passed, and rather than pull the interview to a halt, Hugh let them talk freely. Violet didn't have many visitors after all.

Miss Townsend stood up with a shock. "Oh my, look at the time! I do think I have taken up too much of your time Violet. I could come back again if this would be helpful for your assignment? Do you have more questions to ask?"

Violet nodded. "I have lots more questions. I would like that very much."

She organised the time with Daisy on her way out.

"Oh Mr Marcum, that was wonderful! She knows so much. Who knew Miss Townsend was such a chatterbox? When I used to go into the shop, she seemed so quiet..."

"Perhaps Violet, you allowed her to talk about her passion."

A look of perfect contentment settled over Violet's face, and that had Hugh smiling all evening.

* * *

"I want to show you something," said Violet with a bashful turn of her head as Mr Marcum settled in for her lesson.

"Oh really? That sounds back to front, or upside down... like pineapple cake. The pupil is showing the teacher."

"I got the idea from Miss Townsend. Daisy, can you get my... book?"

She came and stood by the head of The Lung. "You want me to get your... book? *The* book?"

Violet nodded. "Yes, I want to show Mr Marcum. Don't you think I should?" she asked, doubt washing over her voice.

"Oh. Well.... why not? He is your teacher... but..."

"Why don't you let me have a look and I will see if I am a suitable person to give an opinion?"

"Well..."

Daisy went over to the sideboard and placed a closed sketch pad on the stand by Violet's head.

"Can I open it?" he asked.

Violet was not so sure now. "Well... Okay..."

Hugh took it down and turned the cover. The pages were filled with rather crude drawings of figures and dresses and outfits. "Did you do these, when you were sitting out?"

"No... I draw to pass the time while I am in."

"Oh. How?"

"I hold the pencil in my mouth."

"Violet! This is incredible! What an innovative way to use your talent. Congratulations! You have really captured something with these drawings."

"Huh. You think so? I like having something to do. Daisy said if I did my exercises, I could have some drawing time. We made a trade. Gabe made another mouth-thingie... to hold a pencil better, because it needs to be a bit longer. The first one didn't work very well..."

"You and your family have incredible persistence in finding solutions to obstacles, don't you?" He turned to Daisy. "Can I ask you a question?"

She shrugged and nodded. "If you were looking for a new outfit, would you wear something like this?"

"Well... perhaps..."

"Okay... which design do like best out of this collection? Is it this one... or the one that looks like a nurse's uniform?"

Daisy picked up the book and turned the pages thoughtfully. She pointed to a sketch with a broad skirt. "I think I like the style of this one. The lines of the collar and the lapels are modern, and it is a little bit bold."

"Hmm... modern and bold it is. Your next assignment, Violet, will be the major one for this term. You are to take this concept sketch... the one Daisy chose and refine it. Make it into something as if Daisy was actually your customer and she was going to wear it. The lines will need to be well defined... crisp like a magazine. I will see if I can borrow some water-paints, and then you can add colour. I am guessing we will need to practice using a paintbrush, but we can do that during our lesson time too. You will need to interview your client, which is Daisy, to research what colours and fabrics she likes. And you might need to ask some questions of Miss Townsend from a dressmaker's point of view. Your challenge is to get the picture out of your head and onto the paper as accurately as possible."

Daisy followed him to the door. "Mr Marcum, did you have this planned all along when you brought her those magazines?"

He looked at her and smiled. "I am tempted to say that I masterminded this right from the start. I would do that if I thought it might buy some credibility in your eyes. But truth-be-known I am flying by the seat of my pants. My go-to assignments have always been written compositions and science projects. How do I engage someone's learning when analysis through an essay is impossible? Of all the students that I teach, I find I pray most while I am sitting by Violet's bed. I think it is because she is so confined. At her age she is supposed to be embracing the grand possibilities of life... and I struggle to consider how to start with recapturing even the smallest portion of this. But these sketches brought a light into her eyes. Sometimes my plan is as simple as following that light." They spoke a little bit further before he left.

* * *

They sat and did Maths. Violet completed a work sheet pinned to her stand. Hugh had compiled problems related to lengths of fabric, cotton reels and measurements.

As he was packing up, he asked, "How are you going with your other assignment. Do you have any questions you want to ask about that?"

"There is one thing..."

"Oh?"

"You said I needed to research types of fabrics and colours. But I don't have access to any types of material other than bed sheets."

"Hmm. That is a problem. How do you think you can go about this?"

"Well... I don't know. I want to look through some of Miss Townsend's fabric sample books. That's what I need."

"Do you have access to those?"

"Well no. Obviously not."

"Then... given you don't have that, what could you do instead?"

"Maybe I could borrow the sample books so I could go through them slowly..."

"You certainly could ask, but I imagine such a book would be required to stay in Miss Townsend's shop for when her customers come in. She might bring it in when she visits, but do you think it is likely she would let it off her shelf for an extended time for you to study?"

"She might, if you ask her."

"Violet, this is your assignment. You are required to work this out, using resources and people, other than me."

Violet frowned and turned her head towards the wall. "I don't know what else to do. You want me to fail this assignment!"

"What I want, is for you to think creatively about possible solutions. I know you are frustrated Violet. But use that frustration to find a work-around to this problem. That is as much a part of the assignment as the drawing itself. You are a clever, intelligent young woman. I know you can find a practical solution, while still being realistic about what you have access to."

Daisy had a habit of walking Mr Marcum to the door. "That was rough," she said with a frown.

"In what way?"

"You should have offered to help, rather than just leave her wallowing!"

"Nurse Galloway, listen to yourself. If you did all of Violet's stretches for her, how would that help her muscles to stay flexible and build strength?"

"But she already has so much to deal with."

"I cannot disagree. She has."

"Then you should help her! It was a simple enough thing that she asked of you."

"True. I could do that. As could you."

"You are as ruthless and cold hearted as I have suspected all along!"

"It is a risk, I concede. I have a dozen workable ideas that could fix this quite simply. As do you, probably. But I am going to ask that you let her do this herself."

"Oh, you are cruel."

"I doubt you really believe that. It doesn't matter how grand my ideas are, because if she finds one solution herself, even if it doesn't work particularly well, that will be the trump card every time. It is my hope that she will use her frustration to nut out a creative way through, not shut her down. She is always going to have roadblocks in her life... especially now. You are helping her to manage that with her physical exercises. Her confidence had taken a huge hit, but it is building up again. She needs practice in talking and articulating what she needs. I want her to stretch those muscles by encouraging her to find her own solutions... however unformed and clunky those ideas might start out to be. If I solve this for her, she won't have to find her own way."

* * *

7

"Okay... let's get started. Good afternoon ladies and gentlemen... well it is almost evening. So, good evening. I apologise it is so late. It has been quite a week. All the Academy students have been showcasing their work to their family since the restrictions on school assemblies mean we can't do our annual concert, as we normally would. Your showcase is the final one for all the Academy students. Please congratulate our students for their hard work this term." There was an enthusiastic burst of applause from the chairs that were lined up around the living room.

"I have even made an item of my own to Showcase. I've cooked another upside-down pineapple cake for supper. That will be my contribution for show-and-taste, when we are finished. So, let's begin. Youngest first...which would be you, Miss Lucia Trimboli. Lucy... I believe you have a drawing?"

Faith helped her four-year-old daughter pin up her colourful nondescript scribble with great care. There was a story about a bird that went with it. Everyone clapped.

"Edith-Rose, would you like to show your painting now?"

She proudly stood and circulated with her art along the line of chairs. "Can you tell us the story of this picture?"

"I painted our farm animals using my handprints... see this is Sparkle the cow, and Sliced-Ham, with her little piggies and the chooks... and Major, the horse." She matched her hand to the prints, and they congratulated her on her clever artistic efforts. Joe thought the horse looked like a camel and Mr Marcum talked about the colours she had mixed.

"That is beautiful Edith-Rose. Well done." He directed her to pin it up on the board that stood on an easel at the centre of the room.

"Gus... what do you have for us?"

He held up his drawing. "This is the farm and the town houses... that is Mum with Edith-Rose and Jimmy and Joe. This is Daisy, and next door is Faith and Gabe and baby Lucy."

"I'm not a baby! I'm four years old!" Lucy declared definitely.

"Where is Philip and me?" asked Violet. "It's like we don't exist."

"You are in the house where Daisy is, see there... in The Lung." She unapologetically pointed to an obscure blob in the window of the house, and then she pointed to a speck in the sky. "And that is Philip... he's tiny because he is a long way away.... like stars are a long way away..."

Then he pinned it next to Edith-Rose's drawing.

"Joe, your turn. Come and show what you have prepared."

"I made a marble run. This is how it works." He poured a couple of marbles into the cardboard construction of repurposed cylinders and raced them to the bottom of the maze.

"That ain't science," said Jimmy disgustedly. "That's just fun pretending to be science."

"Okay Joe, can you reassure your audience about the science we talked about, behind your marble run?"

"Dunno... Gravity, balance, friction maybe. But really... yeah... it's mostly fun!" he admitted with a twinkle. And he dropped another marble into his construction.

"You are absolutely right. Lots of applied physics in your construction. Science can be fun."

"Jimmy, I'm assuming you have a serious presentation for us... without any fun."

"I've made a working model of lungs. Daisy showed me her books to explain why Violet's lungs don't work and why she needs the machine. This is the way the lungs are supposed to work when our muscles are strong. When they ain't, the machine does it for her."

"Can you demonstrate your model, Jimmy?"

"Yep. When I pull on this diaphragm here... the balloons inside the bottle inflate. See... that is serious science."

"Very serious. There is room for both serious projects and fun projects. You've done an excellent job working on this model." Jimmy looked sheepish and didn't move. "Is there something else you would like to share about your model Jimmy?"

"Maybe. But not this one. I did another one."

"You did extra work, all by yourself?"

"Yes Sir. I made another model."

That was suspicious. "Now you have my attention. What subject did you choose for your other presentation?"

"Science."

"And which field of science did it focus on? Biology again?"

"Geology."

"Oh. Geology?" Mr Marcum looked dubiously at the mischief in his eyes. "Okay... well let's see it." He knew Jimmy was clever and rarely did he feel he worked to his capacity. He also knew boredom channelled Jimmy's energy in crazy ways.

Jimmy bounded outside and brought in a board piled with a dried mud construction. Dry twigs were poked into the mud for trees. Some of the mud caked off and landed on the floor.

Hugh looked at it with interest. "A mountain?"

"Yes Sir. But not just any mountain. A Volcanic mountain. Geophysicists have been studying volcanos for centuries. I drew a cross section of the geological strata here...". He pinned up a diagram and stood there very smug that he got the words right.

Faith stood up eyeing the mud on the floor. "Perhaps we need a drop-sheet."

"Maybe... since it's going to erupt."

"Erupt! Jimmy!" Sal quickly jumped up. "This is not a good idea." He hadn't made a volcano; it was probably a bomb. "Outside. Now!"

Faith frowned. "This is terrible! Don't even think about it!"

Daisy agreed. "Get it out! Jimmy!"

"Nobody trusts me. It just means Violet misses all the fun. She is always missing out," objected Jimmy. "How come Joe can do fun stuff and that's fine. But when it is me, I'm just causing trouble. There's no way that is fair!"

Daisy stood by her mother. "You are not going to let a volcano loose inside my house!"

Violet spoke up. "Can't he just do it on the porch? I could see it if someone moves the mirrors."

"Not if it explodes!" said Daisy.

"Jimmy, can you reassure your family, your construction will not be dangerous?"

He shrugged. "Sure."

"Not convinced," said Daisy and Faith in unison.

"What if we move the table from the porch into the yard? Violet can see if move the mirrors. More science. Does this have the approval of all the necessary authorities?" said Mr Marcum quickly looking around the room. There were reluctant nods and uncertain looks. "Jimmy, explain what you have chosen to activate your volcano? Is it a chemical reaction?"

"I'll set it up and show you."

A table was moved off the porch into the yard. Jimmy's model was carefully placed in the centre of the table. Mirrors were maneuvered and adjusted to Violet's line of vision, so she could see what was going on. Hugh opened the door and pulled aside the curtains so Violet could see. The landing light went out. Jimmy disappeared from sight.

Daisy gasped, "I can smell burning!"

Suddenly there was an eruption of sparklers, firecrackers, and tom-thumbs. A fireworks fountain gushed from the top of the model spewing colourful sparks and fizzles all over the yard and onto the porch. As the eruption faded as the sparklers fizzled to a stop. There was a collective sigh inside the room. Suddenly the base of the volcano blew apart, and a section of table sheared off and landed hard on the decking with thump. Joe cheered; Gus clapped; Edith-Rose hid behind Sal's legs and Lucia cried. Faith picked her up and soothed her. Violet grinned, tears leaking from her eyes. Daisy gently dabbed her tears. Mr Marcum was silent for a long time after the display had subsided. Gabe shook his head, supressing a grin, and went out onto the porch to pick up the timber fragments. He made Jimmy check there were not any spot embers that might simmer dangerously and burn down the house.

When they came back inside, they bombarded Jimmy with questions about how he had put it together and where he sourced his stash of fireworks. Hugh steered him back to how his model correlated to a real volcano. He answered a few questions with a shrug, and deferred to his younger brother's wisdom. "Dunno really... it was mostly fun," he said with a grin.

Hugh shook his head. "I cannot say that I have had such an eventful showcase evening... ever."

Joe started looking around for food. Hugh stood up quickly. "Although that is a hard act to follow, we still have Violet's showcase item. Please. Everyone be seated. Violet, can you tell us what you chose for your item?"

She was uncertain. "I was going to show the painting I did for my assignment. You promised to bring it when it was marked... but I haven't got it back yet."

"Oh yes of course. I remember now. I did bring it. Daisy! Can you grab Violet's book from my briefcase please? It is in the spare room."

"Sure..."

There was a long pause as she left the room. He raised his eyebrows and shrugged. "I'm sorry. While Daisy is grabbing that, Violet you can explain your idea, and what you did towards your assignment." Violet looked a bit embarrassed and turned away. "Violet, this is also part to the showcase. Just explain where you got your idea and how you were able to problem solve the things that were difficult.

"Well... I made up a design... for a dress."

"Okay. Can tell us how you choose your design?"

"Umm... I combined a few ideas that I had from the fashion magazine... and drew a couple. Daisy chose the one she liked the best."

"Part of the task was to interview your customer... and work with her preferences. And you did research on what might be needed to make it up if you went to a dressmaker. How did you solve the problem about the type of fabric you might use?"

"I asked Mum to drop in to Miss Townsend's shop and get some fabric samples from her. She sent over little cut-offs of a few patterned pieces of material that she thought would make up a dress nicely. I did up sample sketches using those patterns... and painted them with water-colours. The red-polka dot was the one Daisy liked the best. The fabric we chose is a dressmakers' broadcloth. It is 53 cents a yard at Miss Townsend's shop, so although it is not cheap, it is a rayon blend that would stay looking crisp. Miss Townsend came and talked the design over with me and said it would make up really well. Besides Daisy looks amazing in bright colours, and she hardly ever wears them now..."

"Everyone is waiting!" he called out.

"Coming! I'm finding it hard to open your case."

There was a pause and then Daisy walked through the door holding the drawing of Violet's creation. Everyone in the room gave a collected "Ahh!". Violet turned her head and gasped. Daisy was wearing the exact red polka-dot dress that she had drawn on her pad. Daisy had changed her lipstick to a matching bright red shade and had put her hair up in a roll, styled like the drawing. She looked beautiful as she walked around the chairs in the room modelling the dress with a twirl.

There was an extended pause as Mr Marcum watched her mesmerised. Gabe slapped his back with good natured thump, and he quickly recollected himself, clearing his throat. "Violet, do you want to add any other comments about your showcase item?"

She gasped again... and shook her head with happy tears in her eyes. "No. That explains it exactly! That is why Miss Townsend kept asking me about buttons and things I hadn't thought of! Oh, it is perfect! This is exactly how I pictured it!"

"Well, it certainly does look very nice. Congratulations Violet. Miss Townsend was very pleased with your attention to detail and assured me this assignment was worth an A+. She also told me she was interested in getting some more of your fashion ideas, so keep working on those sketches."

"Really? Oh, this is amazing!"

Daisy came over and showed Violet the detail on the dress and how it matched the ideas in her drawing.

Faith stood up. "Let's have dinner before we try the cake. Don't want you to spoil everyone's appetite by eating Mr Marcum's cooking first," instructed Faith in her bossy schoolteacher voice. "Your Headmistress insists."

Gabe disappeared and returned with a large tray of lasagne. They all pulled out plates. Jimmy and Joe were sent next door to gather some extra plates and utensils, and they sat around the loungeroom sharing dinner together. Joe ate his dinner perched on top of The Lung. Daisy shook her head. "Joe, get down off that thing, will you?"

"Why? Violet has her own private submarine. I like it up here."

"Happy to swap," said Violet indifferently. "Don't drip your food on my face, you grub."

By then, they had pulled out the pineapple cake. It was stodgy and heavy. "I bet you got impatient and didn't cream the butter and sugar properly," said Violet with a frown. "You can't cut corners."

"Noted," said Mr Marcum with a nod. Sal made up some custard, and they turned it into a satisfactory pineapple dessert.

Hugh helped with the washing up and then hung the tea-towel. "Well, I am away. Congratulations to all the students. Thank you for your hospitality, everyone."

* * *

8.

Hugh walked down the street and stepped into a little Italian milk bar. He looked distractedly at the menu board that listed various drinks, but in the end, he just settled on a coffee. He found a booth, and pushed aside the used cups, and sat down, listening to the buzz of young people talking over the music that blared through crackling speakers. This café was one place that escaped the closures, and he was never really sure how that was. He was just grateful he could buy a coffee that didn't taste like Mrs Barrow's boarding-house mud that she served as coffee. He rubbed his forehead, content to sit and bask in this week's stunning success. He re-ran in his head the film-reel of the various expressions on his student's faces as they showed their work while he stirred sugar into his coffee. He lingered over the look on Violet's face as she watched Jimmy's volcano erupt. The way she had stared at Daisy modelling her dress, holding her drawing as she twirled around the room as if on a fashion catwalk, was priceless. When he looked at Daisy through her sister's eyes, he saw something quite different to the starched protective nurse. These were special moments, when his students' learning came to life. He looked up and saw Daisy step into the café. She was still wearing her new dress and little court-shoes; someone whistled as she ordered a drink. She stepped aside to wait, and then stopped as she saw Hugh looking at her. He indicated the booth, inviting her to join him.

"I wasn't following you. I just wanted to clear my head. With everyone still around I could grab a few minutes by myself. That doesn't happen often."

"I understand. You can choose a different booth if you want," he said with a smile. The other booths were crammed and a number of couples were standing at the counter waiting for a table.

"No. I can sit for a bit." She hesitated. "Tonight was fun."

"Fun hey? Nurse Galloway admits to fun. By the way, I agree with the general impression you are making here. I think you look lovely in your 'Violet Original'. Thank you for being part of the surprise; modelling it around like you did. The look on Violet's face as you came through the door... that is something I will remember for a long time."

"Well, it is okay to turn the antics up a bit when it's family."

"Then I feel privileged to be included in that number."

"Don't flatter yourself. In old fashioned terms Mr Marcum, you are still very much the Hired Help."

"Supported serfdom? That sounds a tad parochial for someone who brings modern expertise to little old Lenwick."

"You can accuse me of being narrowminded if you like, but it is true none the less." She looked over the counter to see if her drink was ready. "Mum had a good night. She is so proud of everyone's progress. She has been convinced there is an ongoing conspiracy afoot to hinder Galloway's in their education. First there was the war. Then a series of unfortunate teachers. Until Faith came back to start the Academy she was quite in despair. Now this public-health crisis. You have given her hope we are making progress again."

"Hope is good." He wasn't sure it was a criticism or a compliment. With Daisy he was never sure. Her drink came out, and she jiggled the ice in her glass with her straw. "Fruit juice from a milkbar... that's not usual," he said.

"I don't like milk. Never have. It makes me sick. Besides, you ordered coffee from a milkbar... equally odd."

"How about Jimmy's little fireworks display tonight? That was priceless! It actually blew apart the table! Can't imagine what would have happened if he'd let it off on in the loungeroom!"

She chuckled and shook her head. "Jimmy has a life-long fascination with fire. He's always burning something. I remember once, he and Joe lured us into the meat house like mice following cheese... and then they locked us in there. Jimmy lit the smoker with us inside! Man, we were wild. Because Violet is so tiny, she climbed up through the top vents to let me out. If Faith hadn't bailed us up after we had escaped, I'm sure we would have murdered them both. Rotten sods. It has always been us against them. They were partners in crime; and Violet and I were constantly plotting devious ways to extract our revenge. The most devious thing Violet could contrive was violating their clothes in some way. For me, I'd try to ambush them with booby-traps in all sorts of places. There was probably not a night when we didn't short-sheet their beds or roll their unmentionables in thistles and burrs. We even put stinging nettles in their socks... which they only wear on Sundays. Our antics made getting ready for Sunday morning church something of a horror for my mother. Sometimes as a treat we'd cook lamingtons but include a couple of selected foam-rubber pieces rolled tantalisingly in chocolate icing and coconut. The boys would always go for the larger pieces, so both of them would predictably get to eat foam-rubber, and then they'd be so mad because they missed out on cake. They make practical joking a family standard."

"I love the way your brothers are so normal with Violet. Your family has adjusted to The Lung remarkably. If I didn't see it in action, I would hardly believe it was possible." He smiled then. "It is nice to meet Daisy, who is quite different from vicious Nurse Galloway."

"Vicious? Oh, I don't think you have really seen me in action Mr Marcum. Not yet." Daisy stirred her glass with the straw again, rattling the ice, and said nothing more.

"Now that positively terrifies me! How is it, that Miss Nightingale brought kindness and compassion to the horrors of the Crimean War, and dragged nursing care out of the Dark Ages into the light of modern science... and yet nurses still have the reputation of being ruthless in their dealings with people? I rarely meet anyone who is not intimidated by your profession, Nurse Galloway."

"I don't know if it is the nature of the profession... or maybe it is just my nature. Perhaps that's why it fits well. Apparently, the name Galloway refers to the ancient, displaced Gaul tribes in Scotland. That is my heritage. Lenwick has always been my home, but just now, I feel displaced... a little bit tribal... a little bit the stranger... and constantly at war in this battle against Polio."

"A warrior Gaul... I can see that. You certainly are a fighter."

"I know I am protective of Violet. We so nearly lost her. Hundreds of kids came through that hospital ward. My introduction to nursing was mind-blowingly horrible. I felt like I was cracking inside... right down into the core of who I am. I couldn't understand how I could be living those stories of a military war hospital in peace time... in my own country. In some way it gave me a sense of solidarity with my Father, because he saw active duty when he enlisted. But what was hardest, is that this is not a warfront overseas somewhere. This is happening right here under our roof. And the fallen were not soldiers who chose to do battle, but children! Their lives are being blown apart by this. And yet no one is collecting saucepans to fund new aeroplanes, or wrapping bandages, or knitting socks for them. It seems that unless there is a family member who is impacted by this, for the most part people don't want to see it. Instead, they complain about the inconvenience of closed schools and movie theatres and cancelled country-shows. They are irritated because they are constantly reminded to wash their hands with soap. They don't understand how horrific it is!"

"I see Violet now... and I wish I knew her before."

"She is still the same person: beautiful and vibrant, and stunningly clever. You are bringing Violet back to us, and I appreciate it Mr Marcum."

"Actually, you have brought her back. I know you have done this literally... by bringing her home. But I think it is because she is surrounded by her family, that she is finding herself again. You made this miracle possible Daisy, and it was immensely courageous for you to undertake it. Your mother tells me that what you have done, has come at a huge personal sacrifice."

Daisy shrugged. "She was getting lost in the myriads of other patients who required care. You can't imagine what it was like in those wards." She kept stirring her juice.

"You pulled out of your nursing course to do this. That was a big decision to make."

"Not really. I could not do anything else. I feel guilty because I was disappointed that I didn't get to graduate. They issued me with a basic nursing certificate, but I had wanted to be properly registered with the Nursing Board. Pretty selfish that I wanted to study, when so many people had lost their sons and daughters, sisters and brothers."

"It is not wrong to grieve a dream. That is just as significant as any of the other things that this disease has stollen. I was angry about losing my job. Another dimension to the horror, but no less important. I wouldn't call you selfish. You have shown yourself to be anything but."

"When it came down to it, I didn't want to do anything other than look after her. I can do that because I am designated as the family carer." She paused, and then tilted her head as if she realised something she hadn't noticed before. "What about you Mr Marcum. You said you lost your job. Is that why you are here in Lenwick? Surely a teacher of your capacity could find something closer to home?"

"I am just one of many people impacted by the epidemic... even if I didn't run a fever. I came here because the rural regions seemed to be spared the closures of the city schools. But then, it hit here too. Your sister insisted that I stay to supervise the students' schoolwork while they are at home. Her approach is quite progressive, and it meant that this time I have kept my job. I had to take a pay cut, and reduced hours of course, but I still have a job, and I appreciate that. Some parents still won't let me in the gate... and I just leave their marked worksheets in their mailboxes... drenched in camphor. But at least they are getting some schoolwork done, so that is something."

"You do know there is no evidence that camphor does anything to keep the polio away. Just like spraying the streets with DDT didn't make any difference. Philip tells me they know polio is not carried by insects, but not much more. Until they know more about its actual route of transmission, we are at the mercy of this. Did you know as soon as my brother finished his residency, he left the hospital to join the research teams in Melbourne? He is determined to be part of solution."

"Your brother is quite the celebrity in these parts."

"Ahh yes. My brother, the celebrated Dr Philip Frazer. He has always been a hero of mine. He's the only one who calls me by my full name, Daisy Hope."

"Dr Frazer... not Galloway?"

"He kept his birth name for his professional registration. Technically he is my stepbrother."

"Huh. Didn't know that. So is Mrs Trimboli is your step-sister too?"

"Faith?" Daisy nodded. "When Violet got sick... Philip made sure she was admitted at the city hospital, so she could have the best treatment. But the place was so overrun, and so completely understaffed, that once she was over the initial stages being there wasn't helping apart from accessing the iron-lung. When we were dealing with the paralysis and damage to her muscles, there were not enough hours available to her. They were actively discouraging the physical exercises that I believe would help her. Philip arranged for Mum to buy The Lung with a subsidy. I had in-home training and mechanical troubleshooting workshops... all sorts of things. You would not believe the resistance we encountered to getting her home. Philip organised the railway transport to get us back here. We had to come in on one of the luggage carriages because it wouldn't fit in anything else. That was the worst trip of my life. They even sent an engineer with us. I was so terrified the back-up power would cut out. But we finally got here. I didn't sleep from the moment we left the hospital ward. It's taken me a long time to recover. I think it was not just Violet who needed to come home. The work at the hospital was getting too much. I was constantly on over-drive. I don't remember a day when we didn't do extra hours, or double shifts. Everyone was in the same boat."

"You must have been completely exhausted. No wonder you didn't want to deal with me that day I rocked up to your house."

"I still don't want to deal with you," she said with an amiable smile.

"And yet, here you are sitting in this booth drinking a juice, while I have my coffee. I don't mind that there was a seating shortage this evening." He smiled and there was a quiet pause between them, while the café continued to buzz.

Daisy sighed and cleared her throat. "You must know Mr Marcum, that I'm not inclined to get involved in something that will never progress."

"How can you so confidently assess whether something will progress or not, if it has never begun?"

"Violet will never live independently. Her rehab is plateauing. I was very hopeful at the beginning, but at some point, I need to acknowledge, with a level of realism, that it is unlikely she will ever walk again... even with callipers. The damage is too extensive. She can only tolerate small periods outside The Lung. She has practiced the Frog Breathing technique, but she tires quickly. Even though she is petite, for someone older who has contracted the disease, this has to be, in every way, the worse possible outcome. It is very unusual."

"What are you saying?"

"I am saying that it is pointless for you to suppose we could develop any sort of friendship. It will not go anywhere."

"Well, you have gone from emphatically hating me... your sister Faith's assessment by the way, not mine... to giving me permission to slather your pristine kitchen benches with flour and eggs... to sitting in a booth at a café, sharing a drink. If this is all it ever is, I am content. It is noticeably better than having you throwing darts at my back for target practice, while I talk with my student. You are a formidable foe Nurse Galloway, and I infinitely prefer to be colleagues, even if we cannot be friends."

"As long as you understand."

"Oh, I understand. Perfectly."

* * *

9.

"Mr Marcum, you have a problem."

"I do?"

"Most definitely." Daisy closed the door behind her and moved further down the path towards the gate.

He looked at her expectantly, but she continued to frown as if she had just burnt her hand and was in a great deal of pain. "Would you care to explain my problem?"

"I would prefer that you diagnose this yourself."

"Seriously? You want me to play twenty-questions?"

"No, no... I mean... this is very awkward."

"For you perhaps. At the moment, my ignorance is bliss."

"Well, not for long." She looked around and lowered her voice. "You should know... that... Violet has a crush on her teacher. She considers herself to be in love."

"Violet? How?"

"What do you mean, '*How?*' I thought that would be obvious."

"How exactly could that be the case? Since I am her teacher, you obviously mean me. I have never given her any suggestion that would be inappropriate."

"Oh, come on!"

"Daisy! You know I am completely innocent. I have never been improper with her. You know this! You have been present, or at least very close by, whenever I have had any contact with her. I have only ever been here in my capacity as her teacher. How could this happen?"

"Mr Marcum, do you really have no idea? You visit her. You are kind. You have pulled her out of an abyss of despair and given her hope. You gave her that magazine subscription, something she has wanted for a long, long time. You have made her dreams for dressmaking come true. You listen, you empathise, you make her laugh. It is predictable that she would consider herself in love."

"Oh Nurse Galloway, I believe you are completely serious! Has she spoken to you about this?"

"Grief no! Violet would never pour out her heart about this. But she has all the signs."

"What signs?"

"The usual. She talks about you excessively. She queries when you are scheduled to arrive next. She reflects on your opinions about everything. She asks about your favourite recipes. I have no doubt regarding the accuracy of my diagnosis."

"Oh, this is terrible! I could lose my job if what you say is true! In fact, I will have to talk to Faith and resign my position. Oh..." A groan, akin to being punched in the guts hit him full force and he doubled over, winded, leaning on his knees. His face turned ashen, and his forehead beaded with sweat.

"No. No. Don't do anything as radical as resigning just yet. Faith will not want to endure recruiting another teacher so soon. It is difficult enough to find a teacher in Lenwick at any time, but during an epidemic... it will be impossible. You must stay."

"But I cannot. Not if what you say is true. I need to leave. Immediately!"

"Hugh. You must stay."

"How? It is impossible! Your sister would never allow it, given the circumstances."

"Well then, Faith must simply not know."

"Oh God. I am going to be sick. Why didn't you say something? If you knew this was happening, why didn't you intervene before this?"

"Well, I did try. But that is of no matter now. What matters is that you have to stay and continue to be available to teach the other students. I don't believe you are malicious, or a deviant. I sincerely think you have a good heart Mr Marcum. We just need to implement some damage control for Violet."

"Nurse Galloway, are you hearing yourself? This is not a good idea. Not if she considers herself in love. She is extremely vulnerable. I am supposed to protect her... and yet I have committed an unforgivable crime and exacerbated her predicament by exposing her gentle nature to heartbreak."

"Just calm down! We need to make a plan. Meet me at the café after six. I have arranged to have Friday nights off. Gabe is coming over to stay with her so I can get away."

* * *

Hugh paced up and down the street outside the café. When Daisy came, he went inside and sat down at a booth, while Daisy ordered for them both. He fiddled with the coaster and tapped his fingers restlessly. "I am going crazy. I can't do this. I won't do this. I need to resign," he muttered.

Daisy frowned. "Shh! Settle down. I have an idea. First, we need to wean her from you."

"Wean? I'm not weaning anything. Cold turkey is the only way."

"Okay... but we need to have a believable reason. A head cold. Yes, you have just developed a *terrible* head cold. Violet cannot afford to catch a chest infection. That is a genuine threat with serious consequences. So you are, as of now, in quarantine... for two weeks to start with. We can organise Jimmy and Joe to collect the students' homework books for you and you can do your marking from the boarding house."

"Oh. Okay. A head cold. I can do that." And he sneezed into his handkerchief and sniffed very convincingly. Everyone in the café looked his way, frowning. Then, after a pause, the conversation in the café resumed.

"That is good, but there needs to be more. I have tried to find an alternative to this next part, and I fear you are not going to like it... but..."

"But?"

"You need to be in love with someone else. Someone whom Violet would defer to."

"I am not going to pretend to be in love. That's ridiculous."

"No, it is not ridiculous. It is the only way. Violet will be sad. She will grieve, but she will say nothing and get over it. If your heart is not available, she will remove her affections from you, and direct it to something else... like her fashion-design work. It is the most appropriate way to give her the space to move on."

"Oh boy. It is apparent you have thought about this extensively. I almost believe you are completely in earnest."

"I have... and I am."

"And how do you suggest I find a suitable attachment on such short notice?"

"Is there anyone whom you're interested in? You have been here in Lenwick... nine months or so. If your heart is not made of stone, someone must have caught your attention."

"This is the exact scenario I was avoiding. I had a particularly messy breakup when I was leaving to come here. But that is over now. I don't want to revisit that again just yet. So, thank you for the offer, but if I need to pretend, I will just say I have a girlfriend back home... that I write to. Easy."

"Hmm. I don't feel a fictitious pen-pal will serve our purpose. It needs to be someone local. Tangible. Visible. Here in town."

"I think you go too far Miss Galloway."

"I go as far as I need to, to protect my sister. I allowed that if you didn't have a love interest, that there is an alternate plan."

"I believe you said you would run me out of town without a reference. You now have the fuel for that particular course without much effort. Why don't you just do that?"

"I have told you why. I have more than one sister in this mess."

"Great. What is your plan B?"

"Me."

"You? How are you the plan?"

"You will fall in love with me. Well not really, of course... you just appear to. That way you are avoiding the house because of me... not because of Violet. I become the reason why it is hard to come to the house. You can do your marking remotely. Faith can step in and do the face-to-face lessons."

"But everyone knows you find me abrasive. You are not exactly subtle. That is not likely to be convincing."

"Haven't you ever read a romance novel? Jane Austin was the master of the conflicted heart... the misunderstood hero... the strong and wilful heroine. We have all the elements right here."

"The only thing I agree with Miss Austin on, in this moment, is the strong and wilful protagonist." He shook his head and drank his coffee. "That... and being misunderstood. Can you really think this is going to work?"

"This is the only idea that seems like it will. I'll slowly disclose your attentions to Violet. She will defer to me as her older sister. You win me... and she gets over you. Then, when we are certain that she is free from her emotional attachment, then... we amicably breakup and life can go back to normal."

He let out a slow breath. "Do you really think there is no other way?"

"Well, it depends."

"There is more? What else can there be?"

"This depends on whether you want to keep your job and stay here in Lenwick Mr Marcum. Faith said your appointment was an annual contract, to be renewed pending appropriate reviews. This is a lot of effort to go to, if you intend to just leave in a couple of months anyway. As inconvenient as that would be... to your students, and to Faith needing to find your replacement, if it is your plan to leave, we might as well just bite the bullet and do it now."

He rubbed his eyes. "I was hoping to prove myself to Faith so she would renew the contract. She has indicated that she is happy with my work. I said to you once that teaching is my passion. That has not changed. I like it here. Working in these difficult times has been unexpected. But it has forced me to teach in creative ways and to re-evaluate the way I challenge my students. So yes, I do want to keep my job. But I want to do it ethically, without jeopardising any of my students. That includes Violet."

"Well then Mr Marcum, consider yourself in love. After your two weeks in isolation, you will need to think of ways to explore your newfound infatuation with me. We will meet here Friday nights and report back on how it is going." Daisy took a breath and sighed, and then finished her fruit juice with a slurp.

He looked at her and shook his head. "I once thought that falling in love with you Miss Galloway would not have been difficult. You have just made it impossible."

She frowned and crinkled her brow. "You do realise that you are not really going to. We just need to be convincing. Violet must think you are. My family must think you are. Outside of that... no one will care."

"I care. You are as cold and as sterile as your dressing trays. I wonder if I can even do what you ask."

Daisy folded her paper serviette into the tall parfait glass that held her juice and pushed it away. "You will. Your job depends on it."

* * *

10.

Mr Marcum sat on his bed. Then he sat at his desk. He paced at the window. He prayed. He marked the papers that were delivered to his door by Mrs Barrow, the proprietor of the Boarding House. He made up a term's worth of worksheets. Then he started on the next. He took his meals in his room... and specifically requested some of Mrs Barrow's chicken soup. He spent a fair bit of time coughing and sneezing if he heard anyone in the hallway. When he went down the hall to the bathroom, he messed up his hair and rubbed his nose and eyes red before he left his room, just in case he bumped into anyone. After all, he knew every truancy trick in the book. The general opinion of the neighbourhood was divided in the case of Mr Marcum. A series of cooking-pots and casseroles were sent to Mrs Barrow to support the teacher while he was unwell; the other opinion was that, regardless of his health, he should lead by example, 'man-up' and soldier-on with life.

Hugh thought it ironic that Daisy Galloway would be his collaborator in trying to retrieve this mess. She had said so herself. She was at war, like the displaced barbarian Gauls, whose name she carried. He wished, in a way, that a relationship with Daisy was something he was inclined to pursue. That would at least make his upcoming displays of interest seem less deceptive. He wondered what it would take to have someone like Daisy fall in love. For Violet... it took nothing. It happened without him even noticing. The poor kid — every time he thought about it, a cold shudder ran down his back. It hadn't occurred to him until now, that he had never seen Violet outside The Lung. Her narrow little face peeking out from the Iron Lung made her seem much younger than her sixteen years. But regardless of appearances, she *was* sixteen, and her teenage heart was tender. He needed to respect that... protect her... and he acutely felt the responsibility to assist Daisy in healing those wounds. After all, he had been the target of those affections.

That idea soothed him a little. He was helping Daisy... Nurse Galloway, *heal* her sister's heart. If that meant he played the part of the unrequited lover... then he would do that. Another point of irony he noticed was that he was playing the part that Violet had unwittingly fallen into. And even he could acknowledge that it was a suitable penance for him to be subjected to. Or revenge. It didn't take a lot of imagination to suspect that Daisy would enjoy every painful moment.

After two weeks, as agreed, Hugh prepared to emerge out of hiding. He reported to Faith that Mrs Barrow's chicken soup had done its remedial work and he was feeling much better. He wrote out a summary of all the students' progress with worksheets and the things that they had covered to date.

Faith looked over his report on the students' progress. "I'm surprised you've managed to keep up with your work, given how unwell you have been. You haven't missed a beat."

"Yes, well, I am back on deck now ... in person, and I will do my rounds of the students to check in with them, starting today."

"Oh... umm..."

"Is there a problem?'

"I'm not sure if you will consider it a problem or not."

"What do you mean?"

"You know Daisy is quite protective of Violet... given her health."

"Yes. Of course. She was the one who insisted that I quarantine myself. I have complied with her expectations."

"Hmm... Well, Daisy has specifically requested that you don't go to the house. That you could jeopardise Violet's ongoing health and rehabilitation."

"Well, I guess that is not unexpected. Daisy has resisted me visiting, right from the start."

"Please do not take it personally Mr Marcum. Daisy takes her responsibilities very seriously. She and Violet were the closest of sisters growing up."

"But I do take it personally. Now that I am quite well, it is evident that there is something aside from being sick, that would preclude me from checking in on my student's progress. I would guarantee that Daisy has not prevented other visitors from coming to see her sister." He raised his brow in question. He wondered if Daisy had a change of heart and spoken to Faith regarding the reason he was quarantined.

Faith nodded and faintly smiled. "Yes, you are right. Violet gets other visitors."

"So, as her schoolteacher, do you suppose it is reasonable that I check in with my student or not? If I can check on her classmates, should she be discriminated against, just because of her immobility? Daisy has always supervised my visits appropriately. She can continue to do so. Surely, as the Headmistress, you can authorise this."

"Oh..."

He stopped as he noticed a look of revelation dawned in Faith's eyes. "What?" he asked.

"Mr Marcum, I think your personal interest in Daisy is clouding your understanding of the situation. Please do not become distracted from your duties."

He had not intended to be so obvious, but this was exactly the back story that he needed to portray. "What are you talking about? Daisy has told me to my face that she does not like me. I'm not inclined to go where angels fear to tread." This was true. "So can I visit my student or not?"

"Very well. As long as Daisy agrees. But don't be surprised when there is push back. I don't want her hunting my schoolteacher out of the district."

"I promise you; I will endeavour to do all I can to keep my job, even if that means getting your sister to change her mind about me. Daisy will see I only have my students' best interests at heart."

Faith smiled. "Oh yes, I believe I was right. You, Sir, are sweet on my sister. You have talked more about Daisy in the last ten minutes than anyone else put together. Not that I mind. But Daisy will resist any attention that she might consider could distract her from looking after Violet. You have serious competition there. Don't underestimate it."

"I... I don't know what to say. I think you are the one who is misreading the circumstances Mrs Trimboli. I trust you don't feel I have been inappropriate in my dealings with your family."

"No. Not at all. I am convinced of your sincerity, and the diligence to your work is evident. Even when you were unwell, somehow you managed to keep all your students on track. I actually think a little social life would be healthy for Daisy. However, if you suppose you can turn Daisy's head, I just want to caution you in all seriousness: it will not happen."

"That strikes me as a dare, Mrs Trimboli," he said with a faint smile.

"It is not a dare. I am talking about my family. I will be honest though. Be prepared that if you insist on pursuing this, you are destined for heartbreak. I have given you fair warning."

That he didn't doubt for a moment. He nodded his farewell and left the house. He caught a glimpse of the curtain move as he walked straight past Daisy's gate without even looking. He had other families to visit first. Plenty of time for heartbreak later.

* * *

Hugh knocked on the door of Daisy's house with a big bunch of flowers. He knocked again.

"Oh. It's you. I told Faith, that I didn't want you coming here spreading your germs around." She said it loud enough for Violet to hear. She lowered her voice. "It took you a while to show up. You've been out of quarantine for days. We have a plan remember!"

"You told me to explore my newfound affection for you. If I was really interested in you, I would pedantically check that I am ticking your boxes. This is consistent with what we discussed," he said quietly. Hugh cleared his throat, and spoke clearly, projecting his voice down the hallway. "Well, I have seen the Community Nurse, and she confirms I am quite well."

"Sister Blaine should have retired years ago, so I hardly suppose her clearance is conclusive."

"And yet she hasn't retired, and her mind is still as sharp as a pin. I brought you some flowers to show my sincerity. Daisies for Daisy. What do you think about that?" That stuck him as corny enough to be an ambiguous gesture of either repentance... or interest. He put the flowers on the hallstand as he stepped inside and took off his hat.

"I think it is unnecessary and you are being ridiculous."

"Then what exactly will show my sincerity that will not risk Violet's health in any way?"

"Hmm..." She turned and indicated for him to follow. She ushered him into the spare room, and pulled out surgical scrubs, a mask, cap and some gloves. "I want you to gown up. You must sit at least six feet away from her."

He said nothing but rubbed the bridge of his nose and looked at her with a smile. "Really?"

She shook her head, irritated. "Just do it. You are not going in there any other way."

"If you insist."

"I do."

He gowned up, applied the facemask and cap. He went into see Violet dressed like a surgeon prepped for surgery. Daisy indicated a chair that she had positioned away from Violet. He noticed Violet's eyes light up as he sat. Oh dear. It seemed Daisy's diagnosis was not as far removed from the truth as he had hoped. Evidently, the gown and mask that would effectively extend his quarantine was still necessary. He sat in the chair, but his words were muffled behind the mask so what he said became an incoherent mumble.

Violet shook her head. "Why does he have to sit so far away and wearing all that? No one else does. I can't hear him."

"Because Mr Marcum has been unwell. And we don't know if he is fully recovered. It is best to be sure."

Hugh said something else, then pulled out some work sheets from his briefcase, and left them on the table. He took his leave, handing the gown and mask to Daisy at the door.

Daisy came back into the living room holding his flowers. "Mr Marcum brought us some flowers." She noticed Violet looked at the bunch affectionately as Daisy jammed them unceremoniously into a jar of water. "'*Daisies for Daisy*', is what he said. How ridiculous is that? But... it is true that I probably like these flowers best of all since they are my name's sake." She paused and looked at Violet. "I wonder if he knew that?"

"Oh," Violet said. "They are for you."

"Well, I think he meant them for me, but we can share them. Flowers do brighten a room so simply..." And Daisy talked about the hours she spent changing the water of flower vases that were brought into the hospital. It was hard not to think that bunches of flowers were an unnecessary burden, creating an extra job on a busy ward, and that she had really lost affection for the gesture because of it.

* * *

Gradually the gown-and-mask routine was relaxed, and Hugh could resume his lessons of applied maths and science, and he encouraged Violet to continue her fashion drawings. Whenever Hugh spoke to Violet, he deliberately tried to subtly weave in Daisy's name or opinion on something. It was arranged that Miss Townsend would come in weekly to discuss dressmaking.

One day Miss Townsend arrived with a young lady. "Violet, this is Nancy Holmes. She used to go to school with Daisy. She needs a new outfit to attend a family gathering for her aunt's birthday, but she doesn't have anything in her wardrobe that fits the bill. The outfit must be a demur combination of modest and attractive. I suggested that you would be a good person give your opinion. I've shown her the drawings that you've given me."

86

Violet asked Nancy what she normally wore and then had her model her outfit up and down the room a couple of times. She asked about whether the new outfit was mainly to impress her aunt, or whether it was to impress someone else. Nancy paused. "Hmm." Nancy looked away and then lowered her voice. "Violet... to be honest it isn't just my aunt. My cousins have a cousin on the other side of their family – so we are not related... and I know he will be there. It seems no one wants to go out with the undertaker's daughter, so I thought it would be nice to meet someone who might not see me that way. Just the same, it is important to have my aunt's approval."

"Huh," said Violet. She knew what it was like not to be seen. The Lung made her invisible. But then she realised that *this* time, Miss Townsend had sought out her opinion. They talked about how, as the local undertaker's daughter, dull colours were always expected. Violet suggested a garment with a sleave, because bare shoulders, although attractive, is considered a little brash in some circles. They would use a modest contrasting colour to bring a little pop to the outfit. "Miss Townsend, did you bring your fabric books?" Violet asked. She enjoyed any excuse to peruse the samples. Miss Townsend produced them from her bag, and they spent a long time looking over them. "I really like checks, but florals are also lovely for an event that is a happy occasion like a birthday." And together they decided on a demure navy background, with a coral rose print, using the same coral colour to accent the neckline and sleeves. Violet was going to do a couple of sketches and Nancy could come back tomorrow to have a look at them.

"Will you have something drawn up as soon as tomorrow?" asked Nancy.

"Okay, give me two days. But apart from Daisy's physical exercises and my schoolwork, I don't have a lot to do. This is exciting for me."

That project sent Violet into a tunnel of drawing. Daisy set up a desk beside The Lung and brought in her nursing books, so she could study and at the same time, easily turn pages, retrieve dropped pencils, or load water colour brushes.

Nancy looked over the drawings Violet had completed. She was amazed and excitedly took them immediately to Miss Townsend. Violet's one request was that she be given the opportunity to see the dress in person, when it was made up. When Nancy came back to model the dress, Violet felt a warm glow of satisfaction all over. Another dress she had created in her mind, was now walking around on a person. Nancy said that when she put this dress on, she felt more confident about herself.

Miss Townsend dropped in later that day. She handed Daisy an envelope and turned to Violet. "You helped a very satisfied a customer, so I want to acknowledge that. This is a commission."

"Really? How much?"

"Ten percent."

"I know exactly what I want to buy. I am going to save up for some proper water colours of my own, with better brushes. Thank you so much!"

"Do you think you would be agreeable to doing more of this in the future?"

"Oh yes! I'd love to. But Miss Townsend, I would never be able to draft up the pattern."

"I have been doing this so long, I just about do that in my sleep anyway. It's the fresh fashion concepts from a young person that people are looking for. I admit my sense of style is twenty-five years old at least. Since Mrs Mirabella Romano left Lenwick to return to Italy, I really have despaired of having local input on tasteful fashion. My customers often want something more modern than the standard designs in my old books, but I confess, I find the newer books and magazines a bit overwhelming. I am quite... Well, anyway, I can see your ideas are well received Violet. Would it be okay if I asked Gabe to frame a couple of your sketches? I thought if I could put them up in my shop, people could see your work and I think that would create some interest. Your designs are good. I want you to know that. I even thought about doing a couple of mannequins to match the sketches and put them in the window."

Nancy's success had numerous girls coming in for advice for all sorts of occasions. Other books from the library were borrowed. Daisy started organising Violet's collection of drawings into a portfolio, according to style, or colour, or occasion. If someone wanted to look at ideas for a blue dress, or a party dress, or an outfit for an official event, they could quickly find something for them to consider. Violet's designs and her mouth drawings were quickly making her a local celebrity. Some of the ladies requested a keepsake drawing, much like an original signature in an autograph book. Every week they rotated a framed drawing in Miss Townsend's shop, and a new dress was made up.

Violet's sadness was that there was no point in having a stylish wardrobe herself, so Daisy helped her develop a selection of headbands with matching earrings, and neck scarves. She could wear these smart accessories, particularly when people came to talk to her about fashion.

* * *

<h1 style="text-align:center">12</h1>

"Daisy, did you ever think that Mr Marcum might be interested in you?" Violet used her exercise time to bring up the topic with her sister.

"Who me? I doubt that is very likely. There are plenty of women in Lenwick... widows from the war, other singles who have been trying to get his attention. I even think Nancy is keen. It doesn't seem likely that he would find our situation at all attractive. There are better options for him."

"I don't think that he finds our 'situation' attractive. But I definitely think he finds *you* attractive." Violet looked at her sister with her brow raised.

Daisy wondered if this was going to be an outpouring of jealous rage. "Does it bother you, that he might be... you know... thinking about that?"

"I don't think he is *thinking*. He is certainly interested."

Daisy shook her head. She had been frustrated that Hugh had been very sparse in his attentions. She had expected more to work with. Their Friday night check ins had been scant and brief as well. Mostly he would say that he had something else in the pipeline, ready to go, and then after they finished their drink, quickly leave. But whatever he was referring to, never seemed to get off the ground. "But does it *bother* you?"

"Why would it bother me? You work so hard Daisy. You should have the chance of a social life. I have my dressmaking designs. But you have nothing."

Daisy sat down and adjusted a couple of the various mirrors that Violet had around The Lung so she could see about the room. "Firstly, you are not nothing. And secondly, my social life will get attention when I finally finish my studies. But okay, I will play this game. What makes you think that he is interested in me?"

"Oh... well... certain looks, comments, and he always defers to your opinion... a lot! He never used to. Since he was sick, he's changed. And I think you are the reason for it."

"That's a very strange thing to say. I didn't make him sick." She paused. Perhaps she did. "Do you think it is a good change?"

"I don't know. Is it? Do you want him to like you?"

"No not really. I have enough to do, and I really can't afford to be distracted."

"Oh grief Daisy... you could just go out on a date."

"I bump into him at the café on Friday nights. That is dating enough for me."

"Oh? Friday nights?"

"I go down there to get a juice... and he's often there having pizza or a coffee. We talk a bit. That's all."

"Huh. I was right. He knows you go down there... and he just happens to be there at the same time... each week. He *does* like you!"

"It's not intentional... I don't think..." She turned away to hide the fact that she knew their meetings were completely set up.

Violet looked at her. "Are you blushing?"

"No!" That, at least, was the truth.

"Are you are saying that you don't like him at all?"

Daisy thought she saw interest stir in Violet's eyes. She swallowed her fear again. If Violet thought Daisy was off the playing field, then she might see that as an opening for her. Daisy had to quickly re-think her reluctance. "Well... I didn't say I was not interested... completely. I just thought that we had enough going on here."

"Well... he did bring you daisies. And he fixed the leaking tap because Gabe couldn't get to it... and he asks *you* about my designs. They're *my* designs, so why would he be so fascinated with your opinion? I know it is not your fashion sense that he is after."

"Are you saying your teacher is neglecting you Violet? I can talk to Faith about that."

"I can talk to Faith myself if I was worried about it. I'm not worried... just things I notice, that's all."

Daisy pulled her chair closer. "What do you think I should do? Cut him off completely?" If that came from Violet that would be convenient.

"No! Don't cut him off. Just give him a go Daisy. Please, don't keep shutting him down."

"Violet... you are sixteen, what can you possibly know about having a boyfriend?"

"I read my magazines."

"Really? Your fashion magazines are the source of all your worldly wisdom? I'm not sure that is sensible."

"Well, how else would I know? Miss Townsend is certainly not going to talk to me about the birds and the bees. I know I'm never going to have a boyfriend myself Daisy, so you at least should have one. Please... I like him."

Daisy's eyes flew open in horror. For a moment she almost gasped at the thought that Violet was suddenly going to bare her heart and confess all her pent-up feelings for him. Violet shook her head and laughed. "No, I mean... I *like* him. I like the way he fits into our family. Remember the end-of-term show-case night? It was so much fun! He made it fun."

"Really. I thought it was Jimmy's volcano."

"Exactly. He didn't get all high and mighty about the mess. You were more uptight about it than he was. Come on Daisy... give him a chance."

Daisy looked at her kid sister's face enshrined in that machine like a metal halo and felt a stab in her conscience. She was only pursuing this charade to protect Violet and keep Hugh from interfering in this life that they had together. Would giving in to Violet's pleas support this plan to keep her safe? "Oh Violet, you really are too good to be my sister. I've always known that."

"Rubbish! You are the one who is everyone's favourite. I would be jealous as anything, if it wasn't that you are the most loyal sister in the whole wide world, and I love you so much."

* * *

Daisy met up with Hugh again on Friday night. He was already eating when Daisy walked into the café. At Violet's insistence, she had on her polka dot dress. Hugh indicated the seat opposite him. "I gave up waiting. I was really hungry. Sorry," he said without looking up.

"No bother." She sat down and scanned the menu. And then placed her order. As she put the menu aside, she looked at him and shook her head. "You know... umm... I didn't think you were pulling your weight with this thing, but I can admit I was wrong. Violet is completely convinced of your attentions. I am impressed that she is really buying it. Even Faith said something to me."

"Huh. The axiom '*less is more*' is probably true. Fancy that."

"Yes well, that means Violet will be expecting something else now. She has made it her mission to convince me to go on a date with you. You need to do something."

"Hmm. I don't see why. As hard and calloused as you believe my heart to be, I am not in the practice of putting myself out there for something that is definitely going to be rejected. That does not even make sense."

"But what makes sense is that Violet is trying to convince me to give it a try."

"Daisy, listen to yourself. There is nothing in this for me."

"You forget yourself Mr Marcum. You keep your job."

"See. The fact that you are blackmailing me, so I can be humiliated is really disturbing. You're truly a catch, Miss Galloway."

"It is what Violet wants."

"I thought the whole idea was to wean her from her own misplaced affections. If that is already achieved, I see no point in pursuing this any further."

"Well, I thought so too... but I was actually right about Part B. As soon as I suggested I wouldn't go for it, she became all doe-eyed again. I can't risk it."

He shook his head. "I cannot believe that you find me so repulsive that you would put yourself in the firing line to ensure I am kept away from your family. I wonder if locking me in a tower would be more to your taste."

"Well believe it, because I have thought of that too," she said quickly. But as soon as she spoke, Daisy regretted her snipe. "Noo... I didn't mean it like that. You're not so bad, I guess. We do need to go on a date."

"Right."

"I just want my sister to have appropriate friendships. You, Mr Marcum, are not that person."

"And I will remind you that I never suggested I was, nor did I ever want this to happen."

"Soo... what are you going to do?"

"Really? You are censoring my gestures of fake romantic interest?" He shook his head. He really had no idea how he could feign interest where there was none. In a small country town, that was almost completely immobilised by a health crisis, he didn't think he would get away with the pretending. People here could sniff out 'fake' like a bloodhound. And just now, everyone was bored and looking at each other through a magnifying glass. Besides, he had no idea where to start. He couldn't just take her to the movies, because the cinema was closed. It was not like he was motivated to think outside the box. Such a challenge is something he would normally enjoy. "If you want this to appear authentic, then that is the game we will play. You will have to wait and see."

"But I need to know if it will be believable."

"You really do have a compulsive need to control everything, don't you? Well Miss Daisy Galloway, in this matter, the gentleman chooses the gestures, and it is your prerogative to accept or turn me down, as you will."

"That is a very out-dated sense of tradition. It doesn't have to be the man."

"Well Daisy – feel free to extend an invitation yourself at any time."

"But that means you would have to accept my idea. I think you would turn me down to make a point," she said with a frown.

"Does it really matter which one of us does the rebuffing? We have already established that is the conclusion of this scenario eventually. This whole thing is going nowhere. This was your uncompromising ruling."

"Well yes. But not yet. First, we have to go out, to make the idea that we are together convincing. Be reassured, I will accept your invitation, so you won't suffer the humiliation of a rejection this time."

"Hmm. Well, it seems I am already humiliated." He pushed his plate to the side, drained his coffee cup, and stood up. "Good evening, Miss Galloway."

* * *

Violet had finished her calculations in costing up a garment, after some discussions with Miss Townsend on the exercise. Now she was tasked with developing a template to make such a quotation exercise consistent. She was nervous when Mr Marcum suggested that Miss Townsend mark this assessment, as a real-life industry trial.

Daisy had gone into the kitchen to make a cup of tea, and Hugh turned to Violet and lowered his voice. "I wonder if you could tell me something Violet. What does your sister do for fun? Or what did she use to do for fun? It seems that she never gets a break."

Violet looked at him and grinned. "Reading. That is what she liked to do most of all."

"Reading is such a solitary occupation. Was there nothing that you did together... as sisters?"

"Oh yes, plenty of things: horse riding, swimming in the creek, craybobbing, or getting back at whatever nasty little thing our brothers had done to us."

"Craybobbing?"

"Catching freshwater crayfish... you know... yabbies."

"Really? Here in Lenwick? Where?"

"There are a couple of really good waterholes at the farm. There are parts of the creek that always have crayfish."

"Oh. Can't say I have ever done that."

"You should ask Daisy about it and do it... you know... together."

"Miss Violet, are you trying to set me up with your nurse?"

"Daisy is a really nice person. She just comes across as tough to those who don't know her."

"Hmm. I think I have had enough contact to know her well enough."

"Just try... if not for you... then please you do it as a favour for me? You are the one who said she never gets a break. I feel bad that she never has time off because of me. A couple of hours on a Friday don't really count."

Daisy came back through the door and frowned as they both went silent. "What is going on? You both look like you are plotting to rob a bank."

Hugh looked at her. "We were discussing some recreational activities that you used to do together. Violet mentioned craybobbing. I have never done that. I thought that might be a Lenwick activity that I should try before I leave the district."

Violet gasped. "You are leaving?"

"Well, I don't know. It depends on whether my contract is renewed. But if it isn't, then I only have a couple of months to really make sure I have nailed all those unique country experiences I missed out on growing up in the city."

"He doesn't know..." said Violet, looking at Daisy in the mirror.

"Know what?"

"Faith is pregnant again. Your contract will be renewed. Guarantee it."

"Oh. Well... Huh, that is good news. I guess..." He felt thrown. It wasn't relief he was feeling. He had resigned himself to leaving. "I still think catching yabbies... crayfish... whatever you call them... I think 'craybobbing' qualifies sufficiently as a unique country experience. And I would like to try it."

Daisy looked at his school-teacher suit. She rarely saw him in anything else. "It's messy and dirty. I don't think that would suit you."

Hmm. That made him more curious. Nurse Galloway and her meticulous attention to clean surfaces used to enjoy getting messy. "Daisy Galloway, would you show me the ropes, as someone who is an experienced craybobber?"

"Don't think that is a word. It would be better to ask Jimmy or Joe. They are experts navigating mud and chopped liver and nippers."

"I asked you. Would you be my craybob guide?"

She looked at him. She did not expect this as his idea of a date. She had thought he would... she hadn't actually thought about what he would do. "Well, I do like a good yabby feast. You know this puts the pressure on us though. We would have to invite the family to share the spoils. That means instead of catching for three people, we are now catching for a dozen... and you will be subjected to a family dinner. We have a reputation for being rather severe on outsiders."

"Hmm. You've taken a relaxing outing down by the creek and turned it into a mission to feed the five thousand. It defies the intent of taking a break."

"Well, they do say a change is as good as a holiday. And if we don't catch enough... it will just mean we serve more potato salad. Okay Violet... you can help Mum organise the rest of the menu for Saturday night. We are going to have a good old Galloway Yabby Feast."

"Guess I pick you up Saturday after lunch? What time?"

"Oh no. We'll have to do it Friday afternoon. Crayfish have to sit in clean water for at least a day to get rid of the silty, muddy taste. Catch them Friday... eat them Saturday evening."

* * *

Every time Daisy went out it was a logistical manoeuvre of grand proportions. Friday afternoon Sal arrived in the Ute with Gus and Edith-Rose, so she to be with Violet. Edith-Rose went off to Faith's house to visit with Lucy. Gus was to join the craybobbing crew. The boys had already gone to the shed and pulled out all sorts of constructed traps and paraphernalia needed to make a good yabby haul.

Daisy bundled Gus into the Ute and Hugh drove them out to the farm. They turned into the gate past the faded sign: "Bottlebrush Grove". Hugh was intrigued to see the place where Daisy grew up. This was a different world than that small room where The Lung dominated everything. Jimmy and Joe had already been down to the creek and laid a number of traps. An old metal tub of clean fresh water on the verandah was already populated with a dozen blue tinged freshwater crayfish. Hugh was as intrigued as Gus, who leant over the tub poking at them with a stick.

"Gus, these critters are quite amazing!"

Gus crinkled his freckled nose, delighted to have someone interested in sharing his curiosity. "Look at that one... his nippers are bright blue," he said, prodding it with his stick.

Hugh instinctively went into teacher-mode. "Yes, see how some barely have any blue on them, and others are a dark sort of olive colour. Those ones have spots; each one is different."

When they looked up, Daisy had disappeared. Hugh found her in the loungeroom, packing novels from the bookcase into a box. "I'm taking some books back to the house. I used to enjoy these."

"Can I help you with this later? The boys said that the best time for yabbying is early morning and late afternoon. We need to get going."

"You go ahead. I'll finish this."

"Nope. You agreed to be my craybobbing guide. I need someone to show me how to do this... navigating mud and liver-meat and nippers. Come on Daisy. We have the company of three busy young men. Nothing is going to happen except the possibility of some fun and clearing your head. But you have to come."

"Why would you bother holding me to this? No one is going to notice, out here there are no witnesses."

"I'll notice. And we do have three solid witnesses. Their stories are going to hold more weight with Violet that anything we say. Even if I report back to Violet that her grand suggestion had you fully engaged... as in... not engaged... not like that... just... having fun. It will be Gus' stories or Jimmy's jokes that will mean the most. She worries about you, just about as much as you worry about her."

Daisy looked up at him. "I believe you really are doing this for her. Well, okay. For Violet."

"For Violet. That was always the deal." It really did seem like his penance would never end.

A wild shriek from Gus had them running. He was sucking his thumb, wounded from getting too close to those nippers. Daisy applied a sticky plaster and then they piled into the back of the farm Ute. Gus clung to the dog while Jimmy drove them down to the creek. He hit the ruts in the track hard, probably deliberately. It seemed to shake some of the stiffness out of Daisy's bones, and she squealed and laughed while they steadied each other, hanging on to Gus and the dog and the various things that had been put in their custody. They arrived, amazed that the equipment had not bounced out the back of the tray, leaving a trail of debris from the house. The older boys dumped a bucket of tangled string at Daisy's feet and portioned off some chopped-up liver as bait. "We're going down to the bottom hole. The top one is yours. Gus, you can't come. Stay here," they said as they grabbed all the traps, slung them over their shoulders and disappeared.

"Oh." Daisy stared after them, and then at the bucket of string and said nothing. She had been hoping the boys would take the lead on this.

Hugh looked at Gus. "Have you ever done this before?"

He shrugged. "One time. Didn't catch anything."

"Okay. Well, given the haul at the house, I think the boys already have the numbers needed for tomorrow night's yabby feast. Which means the pressure is off us to catch anything. Since we don't have to do any hunting and gathering for dinner, we can just do this for fun. What do you think Gus?

Would you like Daisy to show us how to catch your very own yabby? It looks like we are supposed to do that with a piece of string and a lump of meat."

His face lit up. "Yes! Can I eat the one I catch?"

"Deal. You catch it... and we will make sure *that* is the one you get to eat for dinner."

Daisy looked away with a sad glint in her eyes as they made their way to the 'top' yabby waterhole. It reminded her of a more relaxed time... a time when she walked this very same track with her dad talking and laughing about good yabby hunting techniques. She could hear his voice as he ruffled her hair affectionately. "The art of Craybobbing is an ancient craft..." he had said in his rich voice. Hugh dumped the buckets in the shade. Daisy pulled out the tangle of string and portioned off a length, cutting it with a pocketknife. She tied it to a stick and a piece of meat to the end. Then they surveyed the bottom of the waterhole for tell-tale yabby holes. "The crayfish used to be all along here. Okay... see there... where it looks like someone has poked a broom handle into the mud. That is what we are looking for. We dangle the string in the water near those holes to see if we can lure them out... and when they attach themselves to the bait... you gently pull them close to the shore. Then we scoop them up with this net."

"Sounds impossible. But we will try. Our job Gus... is to catch your very own yabby for dinner."

They made up a few lines... attached the bait... and dangled them in the creek. And Daisy poked the sticks into the muddy bank, lined up like a picket fence. The water was calm and clear, and they could see the bottom of the waterhole. They scanned the water for any movement. "How long before they come out."

"Could be hours... not always. This is why I brought a book," she said, as she settled back and opened the pages.

"Oh." Hugh looked at her, and went to object, but then decided that if reading a favourite old book by a beautiful waterhole on a lazy warm afternoon... was Daisy's way of having a break, then that was ultimately the mission Violet had set for him. "Gus and I will go back down the creek and see what we can find. Call us if you get any nibbles."

Daisy nodded and waved them away. She could hear Hugh and Gus as they disappeared into the background. She listened to them for a moment, and thought the sound of them exploring and laughing was calming... satisfying even. Then she turned the page and went to visit some old friends within the pages of her book whom she hadn't spent time with for a long time.

When she finally looked up, she saw an army of crayfish helping themselves to dinner. A couple of the sticks had been pulled from the ground. Another couple of strings were now devoid of their bait. Daisy urgently called out, and Hugh and Gus came running. They stared at the mud the crayfish had stirred up, and Gus went to dive in. Daisy quickly pulled him back. "Gently, gently, catches the craybob," she cautioned. "Fast movements send them into hiding again. We have to coax them out unawares." Gently, gently... they pulled the string towards the bank. Focused. One flicked his tail, and disappeared into the murky mud he stirred up to hide behind. But the lure of tasty liver-bits had another couple of crayfish determined not to let go of the loot they had secured. With a final jerk and a poised net, they finally landed one. They congratulated Gus as they delivered it into the bucket, avoiding his nasty nippers. Then they went back for another. They landed three in quick succession.

The hunt continued... somewhat less successfully after that, but in the end, they had five fat crayfish in their bucket, and a lot of mud on their clothes. Hugh smiled in admiration at a particular smear on Daisy's nose and decided not to tell her it was there. By then it was getting late, the other boys had not appeared, so they took their things, piled into the farm Ute, and went back to the house to drop off the rewards of their expedition. Hugh drove the farm Ute back to Daisy's house and delivered Gus over to her mother. He stayed for a bit, listening to Gus tell Violet all the exciting tales of their grand hunt, and how Daisy got mud on her nose. The light in Violet's eyes told him, he had been right. It was worth it.

* * *

<h1 style="text-align:center">14</h1>

Violet was excited about the meal she had planned with her mother. She directed from The Lung and had everyone on task to complete the preparations. Hugh rocked up early to help get things ready. There were salads aplenty. A couple of trestle tables had been positioned so Violet, in her lung, had her place the table. The wide doors had been opened so the long tables extended out onto the deck. Hugh looked impressed at the way the room was set. This family always included Violet; she was never left out.

Jimmy whistled as they pulled up in the Ute outside. Gabe helped the boys haul the tub onto the porch. Gus had his five crayfish marked with string around their claws. He decided he want to keep the first one he caught as his very own pet. It had stunning blue coloured claws. Gus officially gave the creature a life-pardon and put it in a fresh bucket of water. Joe said he could see the yabby weeping tears of joy since his life was spared and dramatically helped Gus choose a name: '*Claw-face Bob*', which was always to be said with a growl and a scowl. Once the exonerated crayfish's name was decided, Gus visibly brightened up and showed Violet the other crayfish he caught.

As the yabbies went in the boiling vat on the stove, Violet was given the responsibility of timing three minutes exactly. That was the rule. She called out the time and like a Chinese Whispers game, the call was passed on down the line to the kitchen, and then they were fished out of the boiling water onto the platter that was passed back down the line to the table. Hugh raised his brow when he saw the cooked crayfish miraculously turned bright orange. The next batch went in, and Violet started watching the clock again. The haul the boys had secured overnight was so great this had to be repeated four times. The explanation being that the saucepan on the stove was not as large as the cast iron pot Dad would put over an open campfire at the farm. The salads were carried to the table. Everyone sat. Gabe said grace, and the feast began.

Gabe brought over his special craybobbing dipping sauce made from his Nonni's famous recipe; it was a mix of his family's Italian tomato-sauce combined with Nonni's own egg-mayonnaise, with a splash of chilli sauce. Hugh agreed that it was the best dipping sauce ever tasted.

Everyone was tasked with portioning off one of their claws and peeling it for Violet. The process of cracking and peeling and eating and laughing and sharing and helping was underway. Gus allocated one of his personal crayfish to Violet and started dismantling it for her. Hugh helped him finish the job. In the end Violet shook her head, overwhelmed by the amount food. Daisy put the sweet crayfish flesh in the fridge for tomorrow. Anything she enjoyed eating this much, was guarded carefully.

At the end of the evening, Faith, Gabe and Lucia went home next door, Sal and the kids left exhausted, Hugh was finishing washing up in the kitchen. He came into the living room with a tea-towel slung over his shoulder. The rhythms of The Lung became a type of white noise, like the buzz of the radio when it wasn't tuned-in properly. Daisy was staring at Violet in The Lung where she was dozing off with a very peaceful smile on her face.

Her hair was held back with a pretty head band. Daisy gently reached out and removed it.

"She has had the best day. Thank you for organising this."

Hugh pulled up a chair and sat beside her. "You're welcome... although you did most of the organising. And you... did you have a good time?"

"I did. I get so caught up in the responsibility. Having a strict routine is the only way I know how to survive it."

"I understand routine, but it's not meant to own us. I'm glad you've had a chance to do something different. I certainly won't forget my inaugural Bottlebrush Grove craybobbing expedition. I had a good day too." He stood up and gathered his coat. "I'll see you on Monday, for school."

* * *

15

Daisy woke to the crash of thunder and the shutter at the window banging loudly. She got up and closed it hard against the wind. The house seemed to groan and creak all over. The room lit up with brilliant flashes of lightening. Daisy turned the light on in the hallway. Violet was awake, so she flicked on the light in the living room, and then went to make Violet a warm cup of milo. She sat with her own cup of weak tea and positioned Violet's cup and straw within reach of her mouth. Together, they counted the seconds between the flashes of light and the crash of thunder.

They talked for a bit. The light buzzed brown for a while and then flickered. Daisy looked around concerned. The Iron Lung groaned, and then cut back in when the power came fully on again.

There was a tremor in Violet's voice. "Daisy... what if the power goes out. What if... I can't..."

"Shh. It's okay Violet. We have the back-up power we used on the train. I'll just get Gabe to start the generator if we need to. You'll just frog-breathe until we get it going. It'll just take a short time. We sit out of The Lung every day. You're good at it now. I'll go and get some candles, so we won't be in the dark if it happens."

The wind howled harder. Lightening flashed and then a crack of thunder rattled the glass almost at the same moment. They both jumped. The lights went out and the Iron Lung stopped whirring and the whooshing went silent.

The still silence after that clap of thunder was eerie. Daisy quickly jumped up. She could not remember the last time she had not heard that Iron Lung wheezing its breaths. She heaved opened the iron casing. "Violet, I'm here. Remember we've practiced your Frog breathing. Just like I said... you keep doing that, until we get it fired up, and The Lung comes back on. This blackout won't last too long, I'm sure. You have to consciously take every breath now. Just like we practiced... just like a frog... gulp, gulp, gulp... now push down the air with your tongue. Remember why they call it glossopharyngeal breathing... gulp, gulp, gulp. Keep going. Keep going. I'm not leaving. I'm just going to light the candles, and ring Gabe, to start it up. Then he can give us a bit of an idea whether the whole street is out, or if it is just our place that is affected by that lightning strike." She picked up the phone and rattled the handpiece. It was dead.

There was a loud knock on the front door. "See, he's here already. You just focus on breathing... you can do this. Gulp, gulp, gulp." Daisy ran to the door, but it was not Gabe who stood there, but Hugh, drenched from the rain. She shook her head in panic. "The power is out. Go and get Gabe. I need him to start the generator. Violet tires easily. I don't want her having to do this on her own, any longer than she needs to."

Hugh spun around, jumped the fence, and bounded up the back stairs, pounding on the door. He quickly returned with Gabe. They checked the fuel, but the generator would not start. Gabe covered himself in his heavy raincoat and hung an old-fashioned lantern on a nail so he could see. He lugged his workshop tools over to work on it. Hugh checked the power-box and changed the fuse. The whole street was down... if not more. Eventually Gabe stood up. "I'm going to get Brian to have a look at it. I'm not getting anywhere."

Hugh returned to the living room. He shook his head. "Gabe's gone down to the garage to grab the mechanic. Sorry... I'm dripping on the floor."

"There's a towel in the cupboard and hospital scrubs in the spare room if you want to change. They are dry."

Hugh draped his wet clothes over a couple of chairs in the bathroom.

"We haven't done frog breathing much longer than half an hour before, mainly for a shower and morning bed changes. A bit longer when they come out to do services on the machine." Daisy lined up the hand respirator bag and tubing. "Violet, you're doing well. We'll give you a break by using the hand-bag. Let us know when you are ready." Violet blinked twice. "Okay. Our turn. Remember we strap the mask to keep a good seal around your mouth. Now I will use the bag. Okay Violet... time to have a rest." They worked together, focused, watching the rise and fall of her chest, talking as Daisy squeezed the bag... wondering about the extent of the power outage and Brian's progress with the generator. "Now I'll swap with Hugh, and he can bag for a bit." Hugh looked terrified, but Daisy came in beside him and put her hands over his. "Rhythmic, slow, gentle. Just like breathing. Squeeze in and release. Perfect. I need to go to the bathroom. Keep going."

Gabe returned with no good news. There was a problem with the generator that needed more expert troubleshooting. Brian was considered the town magician when it came to all things mechanical, and he wasn't getting any life out of it at all. Gabe was asking around, but there wasn't another generator in the district. These were large specialist machines and unless there was a purpose... like life-support, there was little reason for anyone to have one lying around in their shed. Lenwick didn't have a hospital. Also, Gabe had word that the council crew couldn't do much until the storm passed... and the forecast was that more storms were still expected over the next few days.

As Gabe left, the rain started to pelt down again, and drips began to leak through the ceiling. Hugh and Daisy swapped around again, and Hugh strategically positioned buckets and saucepans to collect the leaks and mopped up the water. They stayed together in that little room, huddled around the candle, flickering in the draughty house, breathing for Violet by squeezing the bag, holding their breath when the thunder cracked and crashed.

To pass the time, Daisy and Hugh tried to outdo each other with fantastic stories of other big storms they had weathered over the years. Daisy looked at Violet, "Remember that storm when the big silky-oak tree just toppled over like a twig. The ground was so soft from all the rain we had that year, that the roots just came out like we were pulling up weeds. It hit the chook pen when it fell over, and we were so sure all the chooks would have all been smashed to pieces... but no... they were fine. Just clucking around in the mud and roosting up in the branches of the tree that had fallen into the chook-run."

Violet smiled, blinked twice and Daisy moved the facemask. She gulped some air and quietly spoke. "The black hen never recovered. She went off the lay after that."

"You remember the Australorp rooster Philip bought? You were only little."

"Sure... Phil's pride and joy. Feathers were beautiful... black-green."

"Ahh yes. King Lorpe, Monarch of the Roost. Philip talked Dad into buying that rooster to breed better layers. Even back then, he was playing with genetics."

"I used to dream... about a black dress... shimmering green... like those feathers... I was a model on a runway."

She blinked twice and Daisy positioned the mask again.

"I think you should design those dresses. You could call it The Australorp Collection," said Hugh as he started to squeeze the bag. Violet smiled around the mouthpiece... and closed her eyes dreaming of black-green evening wear and cocktail dresses.

The day dawned grey, and still they squeezed the bag by hand. The report came in that the rain had washed out the bridge on the gully out of town, and access was cut. Their mother couldn't get into town, and the town couldn't get out. In daylight Brian discovered that rats had taken a liking to the Indian rubber that was coating the wiring, and he found another part that was so damaged it needed replaced. He would place the order as soon as the roads were open. Nancy Holmes came, determined to help. She rallied the help of Sister Blaine, to take turns sitting with Violet, so Daisy could sleep. Mrs Barrow brought over some clothes for Hugh and made up the spare bed with clean linen from the Boarding House. Hugh rotated out for a sleep, while Sister Blaine sat with Daisy. She insisted they have two people sitting with Violet all times, one to squeeze the bag and the other to help with anything else. By mid-day there was still no word on when the power would be restored. That evening, there was confirmation that this was a major problem, and that it was not known how long it would take to get the town power back on.

Early the next morning, people were coming and going through the house, in an avalanche of support. Many of these people had not visited or seen the Iron Lung before and they pored over it like a novelty in Side-Show Alley. The saying that 'every man and his dog' had turned up, literally became the case when a little terrier, appeared in the kitchen with its own bowl. The idea of a dog, inside her clean-as-a-clinic house, sent Daisy into a spin. But everyone dismissed her objections, since they all knew this dog had a smattering of Jack Russel in its heritage, and his mother was reputed to be the district's best ratter. The dubious decision to bring Violet back to Lenwick when the community was isolated and ill-equipped to deal with life threatening emergencies, was given a fresh serving of scrutiny. A wave of anxiety about the inefficiencies of town power supplies and the hopelessness of the weather washed around like the water pouring into the collection of saucepans catching the leaks through the ceiling. Everyone had an idea that was sure to fix the generator, the powerlines, and the rat problem. Solutions for the flooded roads, the change in the weather, and the sick cow down the road were all addressed. The lack of progress from the council crew prompted an edgy hint of insurrection. Even the Mayor Saxton showed up and in effect conducted an informal, spur-of-the-moment community meeting.

Daisy stared at the mud being traipsed through the house. One of the buckets catching drips through the ceiling was knocked over, and towels were thrown on the floor to mop up the mess. It was enough that they needed to focus on breathing for Violet, without having to listen to people's anxious if well-meaning commentaries as well. Her eyes started the glaze, and she tried to breathe in time of the bagging rhythm as she squeezed, to manage her frustration.

Hugh looked thoughtful and pulled Nancy aside. Then he gathered everyone together. He cleared his throat and spoke in his loudest classroom voice. "The remarkable thing about Lenwick is that everyone rallies in a disaster. Thank you for showing up. We know you care. However, we need a coordinated response here. Nancy is going to set up at the community hall and has offered to be the go-to person for the help that Violet needs. What is mostly required is help with the things that won't get done while we have to manually operate Violet's ventilator.... like meals... or mopping the floor... or fixing the roof. Please talk with Mayor Saxton down at the hall about what is needed to mend the washed-out bridge. The sooner that is fixed, the sooner Brian can get the part for the generator, and Violet's mother can get through. We love you Lenwick. Violet and Daisy thank you."

Before Nancy left, she wrote a little sign pinned to the front door that she was at the community hall and those who wanted to help could talk with let her about how they could help down there. Mayor Saxton delivered updates on the status of other families needing support and organised with Nancy to redirect offers of help to other needy corners of the community. Families sent over food, which they ate cold... while they continued to squeeze the bag. Daisy and Violet drank juices that the café delivered to their door. Miss Townsend, came in and mopped through the entire house. Mrs Barrow came and cleaned out the fridge.

That evening, they sat eating cold stew again. The dog ate most of it as they manually squeezed the bag while Violet dozed. Daisy looked across at Hugh. "You can go and lie down if you like. I've got this."

"Nope. We stay here together to keep each other awake. We'll take turns to sleep when Sister Blaine comes back in the morning. She was very definite that we should have two on duty all the time. She is another scary nurse. I'm surrounded by them."

"Thank you for clearing out the place today. I was pretty close to losing it."

"Even I couldn't hear myself think. They were drowning out the sound of rain on the roof... and the drips in the saucepans." He grinned. "And I will be honest... I do miss Joe's submarine hissing and groaning away."

"Can't everyone see we are doing absolutely everything we can?"

"I think they do... but they are panicked by what's happening. Their offers are not diagnosing you as incompetent; its more that they are worried how things are going wrong. It comes out in unhelpful ways."

Daisy swallowed hard. "I always have the maintenance guy start the backup generator when he comes to service The Lung. I never even considered rats might be a problem! Perhaps they are right. Perhaps it is better that she goes back to the hospital where they have proper resources."

Violet blinked hard and thrashed so the mask came off. She gulped some air. "Don't send me back. Please! Don't send me back!" Tears choked her gasping.

Hugh reached over and brushed the hair from her forehead and repositioned the mouth mask, as he gently wiped her eyes. "Shh. You are not going back Violet. We will do what we have to, to keep you here. Our minds are just spinning their wheels a bit because we are tired and worried, that is all. But there is no need for you to go back. It can't rain forever, and then we'll have the power back on, and everything will get going again, just like normal. Besides, we are here with you... until it does."

Violet stared at them both severely. Daisy nodded. "Of course you stay. I'm sorry..." Slowly Violet relaxed and closed her eyes again. They looked at her lying in her Lung bed, the top propped open on its struts. They continued bagging while Violet dozed off. The ticking of the mantle clock blended with the constant sound of rain on the roof.

"You're a remarkable person Daisy Galloway," said Hugh after a while, watching the flickering light of the candle faintly arguing with the dark.

"We do what we have to do, that's all. Nothing more."

"Well, it seems to me, your 'have to' goes deeper than most people could even imagine. I find that admirable."

"So, you're an admirer? Careful Mr Marcum, we can't have your resistance to my charm softening."

"My resistance? Oh no Daisy Galloway... pretty sure that's not me. I wonder who hurt you so deeply to make your high walls so necessary? Who did you love so violently that you needed to brick over your heart to protect yourself?"

"No one. That is not even a thing."

"Hmm. I doubt that. Was there some city doctor... a friend of your brother's perhaps?"

"Grief no. Living at the nurses' quarters was equivalent to living in a monastery. We had curfews, and inspections. Who came in and who went out was strictly monitored. Even my visits with Philip were closely scrutinized – I had to have a pass to see my own brother! Some of the girls used to go AWOL; there was a particular drainpipe from the back balcony that was known as 'the fire-escape'. Some smuggled in contraband; some flouted the rules and lost their job after the second warning. Mostly, I was the paragon of a scholarly virtue as a nursing student. I think the most rebellious thing I managed was to take deeper baths and longer showers than was allowed. Hardly the stuff of a prodigal... and no broken hearts."

"Deep baths! There you go - you are an anarchist after all. I have suspected this all along."

She smiled, shook her head, and deflected the subject. "Nancy seems taken with you."

"Oh, give me a break. You make it sound like I leave a trail of broken hearts wherever I go."

"Maybe you do. The eligible bachelor of Flynn Galloway Academy is a local celebrity. Nancy is too a nice person to have her heart broken. We were in the same grade at school. She keeps asking about you."

"Hmm. If that is the case, I might need your help to rescue me from Nancy as well. She is your good friend, and I really don't want to break her heart."

"You don't need rescuing from Nancy. She is a lovely person."

"I know. Kind. Organised. Considerate. Her wardrobe has certainly improved since Violet has been making designs for her. But... I'm not going there. I would not dare put myself in a position of being accused of two-timing."

"What do you mean?"

"You do know there is already an understanding in Lenwick that you and I... we are an item."

"There is not."

"We have regular café dates on Friday evenings; plenty of witnesses there. I am the schoolteacher who is always on your doorstep. I strictly quarantined in submission to your directions even though popular opinion was that a true Lenwickian would tough it out and keep going. And now... here I am helping with Violet in this crisis. And to complete that picture, I evicted the whole town from your house this morning, and you didn't even flinch. It is established... you and me... we are together."

"Oh."

"Yep Daisy, I think you should know. Officially... in the eyes of Lenwick, we are now in love. It must be satisfying to know that your plan has been executed so seamlessly. This was your strategy. It has been accomplished."

She gave a tired sort of chuckle. Her hands ached from automatically squeezing the bag, and she handed it over to have a break. She found some hand-cream and massaged her hands. "Who knew that could happen without me even realising it."

"That's because you've bricked over your heart Daisy, so it is impervious to cracks. It is comforting in a way, because it means I don't need to fear breaking your heart. This makes our friendship sure... even if it is shallow."

"Well, your plutonic superficial friendship is appreciated. I am grateful you are here."

"Or... perhaps I am completely wrong. Perhaps you haven't bricked up your heart for protection; it might simply mean your heart is so compacted that it exists in a naturally solid state... made of stone."

"No need to be mean. I was being sincere. You have made this disaster much easier to manage. I'm trying to thank you."

"You are welcome... Dearest." He said it with a smile, but his voice was tinged with sadness. It was true... the daisy petals would always fall on 'she-loves-me-not'.

Daisy shook her head... tired and strained. "I see you are going to extract a great deal of mileage out of this arrangement."

"Oh, you are absolutely right."

* * *

16

After three days, as the dawn grey was filtering through the window, the lights flickered on. They waited, holding their breath, for it to go off again. But it stayed on. Daisy quickly adjusted the seals around The Lung and lowered the top. Violet opened her eyes, looked around and nodded, blinking her eyes. They turned it on, and it lurched, shuddered, and started to wheeze again.

Hugh gently took the mask away and disconnected the bag. "I didn't think I would say this... but I actually missed that sound. I've longed for its comforting gasping. The house has been too quiet without it."

Daisy quietly nodded. "I would agree."

Then, as if Violet had been waiting for the comfort of familiarity, she relaxed and went soundly to sleep.

"Sister Blaine will be here shortly... if you want to get a jump on the morning and go to bed, I'll wait until she gets here," said Hugh.

"I'm too tired to eat, so I might do that."

He nodded and sat back in an armchair. He yawned widely and positioned a cushion behind his head. He jolted awake to Sister Blaine boiling water in the kitchen. "Do you want a cup of tea before you go?" she asked. "I've missed being able to boil water for my morning cuppa."

He checked the mantle clock and nodded. Breakfast at the boarding house was over anyway. He didn't want to move, and he preferred to blame his fatigue, rather than admit that he was reluctant to go back to his empty room. The solitary confinement of the boarding house was losing its appeal. The whooshing held a comforting rhythm, and he dozed off again. When he woke, the tea in the mug beside him was cold, Sister Blaine was knitting quietly, her needles clicking in time with the rhythms of The Lung. He rubbed his eyes... and drank a couple of mouthfuls of cold tea to wash the stale taste from his mouth. The rain had stopped, and it felt a little weird that finally the morning sun was high, streaming in through the window, the sky clear and cloudless. He stood up and stretched out the cramps in his long legs. "Sorry. I didn't expect to doze off again. Can you tell Daisy and Violet, that I will give them a couple of days, and then I'll be back into our school routine?"

On the way home he went and bought a burger at the café and took it to his room. This thing with Daisy was supposed to be the reason to stay away, but he felt himself being drawn in like a magnetic field. Closer and closer. It was hard for him to describe what it was. It wasn't attraction... as he had experienced it before. It wasn't pity, or any other reasonable motive he could identify which a woman of her situation might evoke. No... it was just strange. But the strangeness was part of the pull.

The next day he checked in with his school families to see how they had weathered the storm. There were varying degrees of disruption and damage. Everyone asked how Violet fared and told how they had felt so hopeless during the storm. It was hard, not knowing how they could help. But the consensus was that Daisy should have the backup generator checked more often, and they hoped that nothing like this would ever happen again. Hugh nodded and said something generic like, "Your prayers were appreciated."

The school term slowly resumed around the clean-up and fixing things. Gabe helped the crew that went around battening down roofs and removing trees. The part for the generator was delivered and Brian tested it over and over. They ran a trial on the change over to the back-up power while Violet was in The Lung, and it worked seamlessly. Gabe built a locker on the side of the house for the generator, so that this monstrosity would always be protected from the weather. A series of rat traps were lined up around the wooden beams and were to be checked every morning when Gabe fed his chooks. The dog stayed and "RugRat" was now part of the family, and it spent a great deal of time under the house. They were very confident that there was not a rat, mouse, or lizard left near the Galloway cottage due to RugRat's diligent sniffing. Life recovered its normal routines and soon the stress of that disaster was hardly referenced anymore.

One afternoon Hugh came to review Violet's lessons and delivered a bundle of fabric samples from Miss Townsend. Daisy came in with a couple of cups of tea, and they settled in to look at the samples together. Daisy would take each piece of fabric and rub it against Violet's cheek so she could feel its texture. Mr Marcum talked through some feedback Miss Townsend had provided about Violet's quotation template, now that she had been using it for a trial period.

"Are we done now?" Violet asked eventually.

"Sure. I think so."

"Well, Daisy needs to ask you something." She looked expectantly at her sister, who blinked uncomfortably.

"Violet wanted me to invite you to my birthday."

"A birthday party? Oh..."

"She will be twenty-one," said Violet quickly.

"I'm only inviting family, so don't feel any obligation to come," Daisy quickly qualified.

"Family, huh? Of course I wouldn't miss it. If for no other reason, there could be a cake with candles and matches, and I am intrigued as to what Jimmy might be able to do with that."

Violet grinned and Daisy laughed. "I will caution him to be on good behaviour."

"Oh, please don't... not on my account. Encounters with your family have been building the most colourful storehouse of fiery anecdotes."

That Friday, at the café, Hugh broached the subject head-on. "What gift do you want for your birthday?"

"You don't have to bring a present," said Daisy dismissively.

"Oh, I think I do, given our current perceived couple-status."

"Well, I'm not going to tell you what to get me."

"But I have to get you something... something that will appropriately align as your boyfriend."

"You wouldn't let me filter your dates, so I won't filter your gift-giving either. Besides, this is supposed to be a short-lived attachment."

"We have already established that it is fully recognised we are mutually involved," Hugh insisted. "We cannot assassinate our affection too soon."

"You want me to tell you what to buy? That is very unromantic of you Mr Marcum, if this is the general idea you want to sustain."

"Well given this romance is merely a construct of our imaginations, then I don't feel the slightest bit guilty. I want to give you something that everyone will read as appropriately demonstrative for your twenty-first. If you approve, they stay deluded, and I avoid the stress. Consider it 'risk mitigation'."

"Oh umm... okay... in the interests of keeping up appearances Mr Marcum, a piece of jewellery might work. Nothing for my hands... not a bracelet or bangle... gets in the way of work. And nothing too flashy, and not too personal. I generally don't wear jewellery... makes me feel like a decorated Christmas tree, but a couple of nice pieces are useful for special occasions."

"Well... that doesn't narrow the field sufficiently for me. Sounds like a minefield actually. Could I have permission to talk to Violet about this... and consult on her good taste?"

"Violet? Oh. I'm not sure that is a good idea."

"I will use the occasion to embed the idea that my attention is focused solely on you. She is the reason we are in this mess in the first place."

"Are you blaming her?"

"Of course not. But if it wasn't for Violet, I doubt we would be here in a café booth eating hot chips and sipping drinks. That is the mess I am talking about."

"Do you consider me a mess Mr Marcum?"

"Perhaps. But we both want to protect Violet, and, as I said, she is the reason we are bothering with this unlikely arrangement."

"Ah yes. On that we agree."

* * *

Daisy went to the kitchen to start reheating dinner, and Hugh took the moment to adjust his chair closer. He lowered his voice. "Those dresses you designed for Daisy... is there some sort of jewellery... a necklace, or earrings perhaps, that would go well with that."

"Oh?" Violet raised her eyebrows and grinned.

"I want to get her something for her birthday."

"Well, I have designed another dress for her birthday. Mum is getting it made up in blue gingham... and I was thinking that white beads would go nicely with that. Not pearls. That would be too much."

"Beads. Perfect. In white. And Daisy doesn't know you've done this? How did you manage that?"

"Nancy is helping me. She comes in for a couple of hours a few days during the week, to help set up my drawing things. It is nice just to discuss clothes with someone who is interested. It isn't really Daisy's thing. Nancy is starting co-ordinating a fashion service... so she can handle all the customer side of things, because Miss Townsend is too busy doing all the extra sewing."

"Sounds like a perfect arrangement."

"Not perfect. *Perfect* would be able to do dressmaking myself. But I can't... so this is okay."

"You are wise young lady, Miss Violet Galloway. Wise indeed."

* * *

"This is for the Galloway girl, isn't it?"

"Who? No of course not. Violet is my student!"

"Not her. The nurse. It's been noticed you know... how you are always hanging around there. More than a teacher normally would. You give

126

her flowers. The kid is just an excuse in my mind." He pulled at the sleeves on his suit that was a little too tight and glared at him.

Hugh took a deep breath. "Well then, Mr Bollinger you may be correct. This is for Daisy's birthday. I was hoping for something... tasteful."

"See. I was right. Nothing gets past us. Just so happens that I got something in. Thought you might like it. Ordered it in special... just in case. Knew her birthday was coming up."

"That is quite some risk you take Mr Bollinger; assuming I will buy it."

"No risk. I guarantee you will. Take a look at this. He pulled out a drawer, extracted a soft satin pouch, and tipped its contents onto a velvet mat on the glass countertop. "This says Happy Birthday Daisy." Mr Bollinger's pudgy fingers were arranging the pieces carefully on the mat. "This is a gift that says 'sweetheart'... especially for a significant birthday."

Hugh looked at it and tried to hold his ground. Unfortunately for him, Mr Bollinger was right. It was perfect. An enamel white daisy chain necklace with yellow centres, laid boldly arranged on the mat. Then, he extracted another pouch and placed matching earrings beside it. "What is the price?"

"Well, this is a custom-made piece... not one of those cheap factory jobs. Eighteen dollars for the necklace, and twelve dollars for the pair of earrings. They are a set. Can't really have one without the other."

"Oh, my goodness! This is a heist in broad daylight! That is a ridiculous price. They are not made of diamonds."

"You said yourself it has to be 'tasteful', and it's got to be personal too. You don't get more personal than this."

"I will give you twenty dollars for both pieces."

"Twenty-five... and I'll gift wrap it for you."

Hugh sighed and nodded. That was far more than he had hoped to spend. Still, it was her twenty-first birthday, and she was supposed to be his girl.

* * *

"Oh Daisy... that is a beautiful gift. Look at the grain of the wood... and the carving! It is absolutely exquisite. Is this Henrick's work?" Sister Blaine caressed the carving of daisies over the cedarwood lid. Daisy nodded. Sister Blaine was right. It was superbly crafted. She showed her how to unlatch the mechanism and it even had a couple of the secret compartments that were incorporated into the drawers. She already had some pieces of jewellery in it, including Hugh's gift of the daisy-chain necklace.

"The timber has a story apparently. My Dad... when he married my mother... my birth mother... because of his work in timber, he chose a special cedar tree, to be made into their dining table. Then, when he married Mum, he did the same thing... but using silky oak. They always made a big deal of the fact they married on my first birthday. And they had the cedar from the old table made into wooden jewellery boxes. One for each of the girls in Dad's life, he used to say... and we were to get them on our twenty-first birthdays."

"This is the wood from their dining table?" Sister Blaine asked gently.

"Timber. Dad was always particular that *wood* is what you burn in a fireplace; *timber* is what you use to build and craft. Since the table was such a special item, they couldn't just get rid of it, so the cedar timber was used to craft these gifts. Dad gave Mum one as wedding gift with poppies and ivy engraved on it representing peace and love. Faith has carvings of lilies on hers – her middle name is Lily. I have daisies... and Violet... Doesn't take a genius to work out what will be on her box. Mine is a little different, in that Mum collected some things… mementos of my birth mother and put them in there as well. Their wedding photo, some doilies that my mother embroidered, and a couple of pieces of jewellery that belonged to her, including her rings. I always like the idea that together… me and my mother were Joy and Hope.”

“I knew your mother and she was remarkable,” said Sister Blaine. “You are much like her in that way,” she said as she stared at the box, and swallowed hard. “That is a lot of family history in one gift. What a very touching family tradition to have.” She quickly gathered her things. “Well, I will be going. Sounds like your teacher is here.”

Daisy nodded and went back to braiding Violet’s hair. “Thanks for coming Sister,” she called after her.

Hugh passed Sister Blaine in the hallway as she rushed out the door. “She’s in a hurry to leave. Is she okay?”

“Well, I think so. We were just talking about the jewellery box. Huh. I suppose she did get a little weird about it. Mum said Sister Blaine always had a soft spot for me because she was at my birth.”

“Well then, she probably has a soft spot for most of the town… since she’s been Lenwick’s midwife for a long time.”

“True. I’m just going to finish braiding Violet’s hair; we washed it this afternoon. Will it be okay if I keep going while you discuss your lesson?”

“Sure. Violet, today we are looking at history again. Did you read that section in Faith’s art-book on how fashion can tell us about various people’s lives by the way they dressed?”

They looked at some portraits in Faith’s book. Violet was particularly taken with a painting of a nineteenth century couple dancing and how different their clothes were. Then they considered clues in a few old photos of various occupations that Hugh borrowed from Mrs Burrow's boarding house. Daisy joined in their discussion, and they identifyed themes of culture, status, occupation, beauty and gender, all shown through the way people dressed. "You know, given that Art History is Faith's speciality, how would you feel about Faith taking your next lesson?"

Violet hesitated.

"She knows this subject inside out," encouraged Mr Marcum.

"I want Faith to just be my sister. It is nice being neighbours, so she can bring Lucy to visit," said Violet.

"Well, all right. How about, instead of her 'teaching' the lesson, I want you to think of four questions you can ask her, and then just have a conversation. It will give you something to talk about... sister to sister."

Faith and Gabe arrived, prepared to do battle on Daisy's Scrabble board. It was a gift that Philip had sent from America for Daisy's birthday. Playing games after dinner on Friday was another highlight of Violet's week. Lucy had some grandparenting time with Gabe's family so they could play uninterrupted. Daisy disappeared to get ready for their 'date' night.

Hugh looked up as Daisy walked in, dressed for their outing in the light blue check gingham dress Violet had designed for her birthday. "Oh my... you look incredible! What do you think Violet? Isn't your sister the prettiest nurse in all of Lenwick? Does the daisy-chain necklace suit the outfit? It has my vote."

Violet smiled. "Apart from old Sister Blaine, Daisy is the only nurse in Lenwick. You are going to have to improve your compliments Mr

Marcum," she said with a grin. She required Daisy to do a couple of twirls, until she was completely satisfied. Gabe hunted them out the door.

Hugh walked her to the car and opened the door. Daisy glanced back at the house and saw Faith looking around the curtain at them. "I think you are doing this quite well," she said. "Your attempts to compliment are laid on a little thick, but they have my family convinced," said Daisy.

When he slid in behind the steering wheel, Hugh paused before he turned the key. "Daisy, I'm not performing like some circus clown for your family. If I say you look nice, I mean it. The compliment was intended for you... not them. I bought the necklace because I thought you would like it, not to impress your family. I hope you understand this."

"Oh. Since you had me vetting gift ideas, I thought... I'm sorry. It is a nice gift."

"Not pretending." He sighed deeply, as if instinct, hoping that the breath would help re-set his internal equilibrium. "Do you want to go to the café... or can we grab takeaway and go somewhere quieter? Up to you."

"Ahh... takeaway sounds good. Where would we go?"

"Let's sit down by the river. It's a clear night."

They sat on a rug, eating hamburgers and chips, listening to frogs gurgling in the marshes, and cicadas singing in the night air. They watched the moon rise, and the light shimmered over the water. "They used to have boats for hire here. I remember rowing down the river with my parents when I was little," said Daisy looking at the pylons jutting out of the water. "This is all that is left of the old pier that had been used as the landing platform. Dad would bring mum here on their anniversary every year... which was also my birthday... so sometimes I got to come along."

"We could recreate some of the history and go rowing together sometime. If I had known I could have taken you for your birthday. Perhaps next year then."

"Or we could just imagine it and save the bother."

"Daisy... would you ever consider... going out with me? Without pretending?"

"That's ridiculous. I am going out with you. I am not pretending. This is me."

"You know what I mean. Do you find me so unsatisfactory, that you would wipe me off completely as a prospective boyfriend?"

"Nothing personal Hugh. I keep telling you that am not getting involved with anyone. Not just you."

"But why? I don't understand."

"I just won't, that's all."

"I don't suppose you can see why I find that explanation completely inadequate. Yes, I know... you don't have to explain yourself to me, but it would really help me to understand. What is it about me that does not work with girls? This is not the first time my heart has been broken by the fairer sex. Please Daisy, help me understand."

"Heartbroken? Damn it, Hugh. I told you up-front what this was, and what it would look like. Why did you have to go and get all messed up over it? By being honest at the start, we were supposed to avoid this."

"Well, I am being honest. And I don't get it. I have a good job. Not high-powered executive status I know, but teaching is quite respectable. I'm not exactly a dullard. You have said I am kind and considerate. I give you daisies and reasonable birthday presents. What is it? What am I missing?"

"It's not you. Seriously, you're okay. But I've already told you, I'm not doing this."

"If this is about Violet, we can care for her together. In many ways we already do. I'm not bothered by that."

"See. I knew it. That alone would send the average bloke running for the hills. But not you. Oh no. You want to stay and help. You know, if I had a sister... who was not under-age, or living in an iron lung... I would give her a recommendation just to keep you in the family."

"Okay. So, I'm alright for someone else, but not you." He shook his head bewildered. "Please Daisy... as a friend, I really want to understand."

"But I have already told you. You're fine. It's me."

"So, you are in love with someone else then?"

"No. Why does it always have to be a competition? I told you... there is no one else. There will never be anyone else."

"Why not? Have you taken a vow or something?"

"Because... well, I'm... If you must know, I'm cursed. I have an omen of bad luck around me. I wouldn't do that to anyone I care about. And certainly not you. You need to stay away from me Hugh. Once this charade is done... go find a girlfriend somewhere else. It will be best for you."

"What are you talking about? How could you possibly think that you are bad luck? Look at the progress you have made with Violet. She is alive because of you. That is hard work and love! Bad luck is not part of that formula, except her getting polio in the first place. You didn't give it to her!"

"You know I have been thinking about Sister Blaine today. You were right. It was strange. As soon as I told her the story of the jewellery box, she started getting really weird. But then I have been thinking. She was at my birth... which means she was also there when my mother died. My mother died giving birth to me. That is my curse. Wherever I am, people die. Dad goes to war and doesn't come home. Others made it back, but not him."

"Daisy, over twenty-two thousand Aussie soldiers were incarcerated in Japanese prisoner-of-war camps. How can you possibly be responsible for a third of them dying? I am so sorry that he died that way... I really am, but that is not bad luck or a curse. That is war-crime! Very different things."

"I go away, to learn how to look after people so they won't die, and we are struck by the wave of this epidemic where there is more death than you can possibly imagine. Over a thousand kids have died from this. It feels like I laid out hundreds of them myself. And it's still going on. My sister nearly dies! One of the reasons it wasn't hard to leave the hospital was that if I got away from it, it might stop. I can't undo this thing that is over me, Hugh. I have tried. I mean it quite sincerely. I've have tried to do my penance. But I am like a rotten potato... that leaks out and contaminates everything around me with the stench of death. Protect yourself... and give up this idea that you might like me."

"No Daisy. I don't like you."

"Well, that is a relief. Because it sounded like you were trying that on for size."

He was silent for a long time, listening to the sound of the night birds around the water joining the chorus of frogs and cicadas. "I'm not *trying it on*, Daisy; It is already done. I have come to realise something... and I have to put this out there. I find myself completely attracted to you. Yes, I would even say that I love you. You are not bad luck. Daisies are the flower for good fortune, beauty and new beginnings. That is hope Daisy... not hopelessness.

God plants good things in our lives, not curses. Death is the curse that Jesus sorted out. It is not yours to carry."

"Well, you can say that... but it sure doesn't feel like it. It feels like I carry the responsibility of it around with me. Why else would my life be so hounded by death? To hear you say this, I feel so afraid. I do value our friendship, and I don't want to lose you too Hugh. It is best you stay at arm's length."

"Sorry Daisy, it is too late. None of us know how many days we have to live, but I will not use that as an excuse to stay away. I cannot. I am already in."

* * *

18

Daisy walked into the church in her red polka dot dress and leaned hard on Philip's arm as they followed her mother down the aisle. Hugh walked slowly beside Jimmy and Joe; Gus and Edith-Rose stayed close to Faith who wore a pleated check dress. She steadied herself by gripping Gabe's hand fiercely. The church was cold, and it was dark. Light from the stained-glass windows, muted and dim, streamed in on the casket covered in all sorts of purple flowers... many of which were violets. Miss Townsend wore an outfit printed with purple. Nancy wore her brightest yellow dress. Mrs Barrow had on a spotted skirt and blouse. The men all wore black ties with violet polka dots. Normally they would not have been seen dead in such colours... but today, today everyone wore something Violet had designed, or had purple in it. Bold. Bright. Brave. Even the minister. It felt almost irreverent to do it, but this was Violet's passion. If it wasn't for the tears, the sombre expressions and the whispered conversations, the abundance of colour could have been mistaken for a carnival.

They agreed on one thing – Violet would have approved.

How was it, after all this, that she would be taken by something that was not Polio? It didn't make sense. They were making progress. They had been winning. Daisy demanded answers, even when the doctor that came across from the neighbouring town was not inclined to do an autopsy. It was found that Violet had a heart defect. From birth. There had been the unexplained "failure to thrive" as a child, where even Doc Mortimer's tonic made little difference. Violet... pretty and delicate... fragile in her looks, but fierce in her ability to love life. Salome had put her daughter's slight frame down to her finicky eating habits. When Philip read the report, he shook his head. He said it was remarkable Violet had lived as long as she did... and certainly it was unexpected that she managed to survive through polio. Their mother had taken some comfort from that. Polio had not won, and in some way, they had beaten the odds after all.

Faith pulled Daisy aside at the wake. "You were right you know."

Daisy shook and head. "Good to know... but I doubt it."

"I mean... to have someone so skilled to nurse Violet through this, it was the grandest thing for you to do. I'm sorry I fought so hard against you doing Nursing. The way you have cared for her... it was the finest career choice... and finest family choice, anyone could ever make. Thank you so much Daisy. Thank you." She leant in with tears and gave her sister a hug. "I know it is right for you Daisy... and I want you to know that I completely support you doing that. You should think about going back and getting your full certificate. It is so obvious you are gifted at this. It is your calling."

* * *

Hugh walked with Daisy down to the creek where the Bottlebrush Grove lined the bank, branches swayed, bent and weeping, over the water. It seemed appropriate. "I am going to leave! I cannot stay," Daisy blurted in a rush.

"Daisy, we have just buried your sister. We have literally just spent hours at her wake. You are in shock. Do you really think now is the time to be making such a huge decision? Give yourself some time to recover." Hugh flicked a stick onto the water and watched it float lazily away. That didn't seem right. It should have been swept under the water in a turbid surge.

"There *is* no time. I need to go back and organise things with the hospital. They have kept a place for me, so I can finish my nursing. Philip is going back tomorrow so he can fly to Melbourne in a couple of days. I am going with him. Even Faith thinks this is a good idea."

"I'm not disagreeing that finishing your training is a good idea, what I am talking about is looking after yourself. If you can't see your way to do that yourself, you need to be around people who can... at least for a little bit. Going back straight away, to live in isolation, to work out more penance, those things are not what you need right now."

"Oh, and you are the person to do that?"

"I was thinking of your family Daisy. They are here."

"They are... and I need to go away to protect them. I need to be far from here."

"You cannot run forever Daisy. You gave up your dream to give Violet her greatest wish... to come home. You helped her live! You were not responsible for her going, Daisy. You heard what Philip said. You read the report yourself." Hugh felt himself tilt. He realised then that Daisy might, in all probability, never let him in. But he needed her to be okay, even if he would not be part of the equation in any personal way. He screamed a prayer in the silence of his heart. An SOS prayer. *"God! You are a God who asks questions. Give me a question to ask, to help Daisy find her way through this!"* What settled in his soul, even gave him pause.

He flicked another stick onto the water and watched it bob as it hit the surface. "Daisy... I know you want to run to protect those you love. And I know everything is still like a battle, but I wonder... where is the place you feel safest?"

She stopped then, and looked up, startled like a rabbit. "Safe? What do you mean?"

"I was thinking of what you told me once... about being a Galloway... named after ancient Gaul tribes... living in a tradition of warfare... the battle that you have been fighting, making gains, and then losing footing all over again. There have been so many causalities around you. It must seem like the war still keeps coming in waves and the assault of gunfire hasn't let up. Those who came home from the War, they all carried scars, and some of those scars you can't see. Daisy, you must have nursed returned servicemen who felt like the fight is still going on around them? How did you help them feel safe?"

"Oh. Umm. There was very little we could do sometimes... but two things seemed to make a difference. Surround them with their mates, and... yes... keep reassuring them that the war was over." She looked at him curiously. "How did you know that?"

He shrugged. "I didn't really. It just seems like you still feel under attack. The things you've seen, Daisy... I can't even imagine the half of it. Could it be that you have your own version of battle fatigue from the war you have been fighting? You've been in active duty without any relief for a long time. If you needed to find a safe place, where would that be?"

"Here, I guess. I feel safest here. In Lenwick. Specifically on the farm; Bottlebrush Grove. Our little cottage... nursing Violet there, made it more like a clinic than a home."

"What makes being here at Bottlebrush Grove safe?" They walked a little further and sat on a log overlooking the water.

"Oh... umm... familiarity I suppose. The predictability of the routine. We have to feed the chooks and milk the cow. I know every weather-beaten tree, every weathered board on the house and sheds, every track, every bend in the creek. It's home."

"Chooks? That's unexpected. Country living without the convenience of city shopping."

"I know, right. But its predictable. We have to collect the eggs, or the goanna gets them, and we don't have breakfast. In the city I would go shopping and be so overwhelmed that everything was just there on the shelves. The choice made my head spin, and I would walk away without buying anything. The other girls could never understand why I didn't like spending hours wandering around department stores. Didn't enjoy it at all. Lenwick general store is much easier."

"What else is safe here..."

She looked at him. Calmer. "Do you want me to say it?"

"If you can say it, it might make it more real."

"Hmm... my family. Mum. She is the constant in my life. And Philip. He hasn't been here for years... yet I don't think of this place without him. While I was away, he kept me grounded. But he doesn't even work at the hospital anymore, so I wouldn't even see him when I go back. He will just drop me off and then leave to go to his research. And Faith and Gabe and little Lucy. Jimmy and Joe. Gus and Edith-Rose." She swiped her tears and swallowed them down. "And Violet. The memories that we have shared. What a change from when she first arrived."

"She really came out of her shell." He shook his head and smiled sadly. "Oh. That was an unfortunate turn of phrase. Sorry."

"But you are right. She did! Somehow, she was not confined to The Lung, even though she was. We made a difference."

He looked at her quietly. "We. That is generous."

"It is true. It was not just me... or you. *We* did it. We all did."

They sat still for a long time... saying nothing.

Daisy eventually looked across at him. "And you."

"Me?"

"You. I haven't wanted to acknowledge it, but you are part of my home here too. I trust you."

He smiled gently. And said nothing.

"No claims of conquest? No exclamations that you were right all along?"

"I'm glad you see me now. I am here... while the war rages. I'm not saying I don't expect you won't go back to the front-line Daisy. I guess you will when you are ready. But I am here. I am the one who will keep the hearth fires burning for you at home."

Daisy stared at him and burst into tears. A flood of pain, and hate, and panic, and fear, and grief, and guilt, and loss, and agony gushed out. He gathered her in his arms and cried with her.

* * *

19

"I solemnly pledge myself before God and in the presence of this assembly, to pass my life in purity and to practise my profession faithfully. I will do all in my power to maintain and elevate the standard of my profession... and will hold in confidence all personal matters committed to my keeping, and all family affairs coming to my knowledge in the practice of my calling. With loyalty will I endeavour to aid the physician in his work, and as a 'missioner of health' I will dedicate myself to devoted service to human welfare."

The graduates lined up in their crisp uniforms, their woollen capes, and stiff nursing veils as they recited the Nightingale Pledge. Then each graduand was called forward to receive their certificate and badge. "Sister Daisy Galloway." There was a cheer from the assembly as Daisy walked forward. A gathered rabble in the back corner, from some back-block bush town cheered and blew party-bowers while Jimmy and Joe stood on their seats, whooped and whistled enthusiastically. There were gasps around the auditorium at the impudence. Some people looked incensed; some looked offended; others looked down at the floor and tried to cover their amusement. There were even a few jealous glances that disclosed they wished they had the audacity to offer such an outpouring of pride and affection on their own graduand. Matron turned to Daisy and pinned on her graduating badge, and she stepped back to join the line of alphabetised graduating sisters. Tonight was her graduation: a formal acknowledgement of years of study and service. Daisy felt a wash of joy and satisfaction fill every pore of her body.

Then Daisy was called back onto the stage and presented with the School's Nightingale Award, a prestigious acknowledgement of excellence in academic achievement and Nursing practice. Daisy's family went berserk once more. Matron pinned this esteemed badge on her lapel, an enamel rendering of a Nightingale lantern. "You have a regular little cheer squad here, Sister Galloway. It seems that your little corner of Australia is gunning for an excellent 'missioner of health' to be at their service."

Daisy touched her starched veil and bobbed the formal curtsy of respect. "Even small places deserve access to excellence Matron."

Matron held herself regally and nodded ever so slightly. "Then do it excellently, Sister," was all she said.

As Daisy was ushered out to have her graduating portrait taken, that little exchange felt like a blessing... a dispensation to follow her heart. It confirmed to Daisy that she had made the right decision to take up Sister Blaine's invitation to be Lenwick's next community Nurse. Daisy smiled. Bush Nurse. She guessed many people would consider that taking that position would be a step down from the other offer as a specialist nurse in the chronic disease ward. But in reality, Daisy knew she was stepping in to fill big shoes. Very big shoes.

* * *

The family looked out over the harbour, and watched the lights on the water, boats and ferries hurrying to and fro. They laughed at the enthusiastic country splash they had made during the sombre little ceremony. Daisy took off her nursing veil, stockings and shoes, and threw them in the car. Joe and

Gus were delighted that those hoity-toity city-folks squirmed uncomfortably while they were cheering. Jimmy was amused that they had managed to defy the heavy dignity of the evening, but he had been bitterly disappointed when Gabe and Hugh had conducted a pat-down before going inside. They uncovered his concealed weaponry of a confetti cannon that he had smuggled in to discharge during the ceremony. He quickly retrieved it from the car boot and blasted tickertape all over where Sal and Faith were setting up their picnic. Daisy laughed and threw her hands up in the shower of confetti, while Edith-Rose and Lucy danced through the colour, throwing bits of paper in the air again and again. This really felt like another V-day. More laughter and cheers. Then they peeled back the bundles of newspaper and helped themselves to a generous feast of fish and chips. No swanky restaurants for this graduating dinner, although the setting did add a suitable atmosphere of extravagance to the occasion.

Philip had come to celebrate Daisy's big moment. He cleared his throat to make a toast to Daisy Hope. They filled up their little stackable metal tumblers with ginger-beer. "To Daisy Hope! Her bright nature and extravagant love, offers hope wherever she is!"

Hugh gulped his drink and swallowed hard.

Daisy demanded another round. "To Violet, who encouraged us all to pursue the love of life to the fullest!"

"To Violet!"

And then Philip made another toast. "To Dad, who gave us all an example to fight to protect that very same love of life!"

"Yes, to Dad. In our own way, we all follow in Flynn Galloway's footsteps. His legacy lives on." There was another cheer. Joe good humouredly made a dig at Jimmy, whose own particular way was to get into fistfights. Their teasing added to the good cheer.

The years to get to this point seemed to recede into the background as the family stories flowed, and Hugh retreated to sit overlooking the harbour. This was their family event. He never forgot Daisy's diagnosis of being the hired help. Hugh felt the privilege of being included, but he didn't want to intrude on their celebrations. He sat in the shadows and watched the play of light on the water. He listened to them joking together and thought how miraculous the resilience of the human spirit was. Who would have thought that after so much pain, this family would still be able to share fish and chips by the harbour and laugh together with such openness?

The change in Daisy was the greatest. She didn't go back to the city hospital to finish her nursing straight away. She gave herself a six-month sabbatical after Violet died. But when she did leave, she made it clear that this was her contribution in the fight against Polio; partly following in her father's footsteps to enlist against a war that would threaten her family; partly as a tribute to Violet; partly to see her dreams come to be... in that order. The ridiculous aspect of this endeavour was that the training hospital refused to apply any credits from the course work she had already completed. There was a new matron appointed who did not feel the need to honour her predecessor's arrangement. Daisy swallowed her pride and started the Preliminary Nursing School again from the beginning. She framed it as 'job security' and joined the teenagers who were launching their careers in nursing. While the new recruits were learning the fifty-six steps to deliver a bed pan, Daisy secured dispensation to engage in dual studies in more advanced nursing care. She was determined to use the time to gain as many diverse experiences as she could.

When Daisy left Lenwick, Hugh moved out of Mrs Barrow's Boarding house, into the little cottage next to Gabe and Faith. The offer of Teacher's accommodation was incorporated into his new contract. Sal organised for the Iron Lung and generator to go to a family in the next town over. Gabe and Faith's little family was growing. Lucia now had a little brother, named David, and there was another baby on the way. Hugh and Daisy corresponded often, and the times she came home for holidays, or he went to the city, were never long enough. They rarely spoke about the ruse of pretending to like each other, and it was only Hugh who ever acknowledged it was more than make-believe.

Daisy came and sat with him in the shadows, looking at the lights reflecting across the harbour. "Thanks for coming down here."

"This is your graduation. Of course, I would come! You had to give it up once before. I'm sure that makes being presented with your certificate all the sweeter. And on top of that - what an honour to be given that swanky little lantern badge. I'm glad I was here. Congratulations Daisy. So proud of you."

"Not everyone would be thrilled about travelling such a long way for one evening."

"It is not just one evening. This is the culmination of years of work." He thoughtfully gazed at the harbour lights. Perhaps she still didn't get it. There were lots of people who loved her sincerely. "Have you thought about what's next? Is there still more battle to be done?"

"It is time to come home. Same war, different front. I will be Lenwick's community nurse. I wrote to Sister Blaine and accepted the job... posted my letter yesterday."

Hugh smiled. "You do realise, given the efficiency of our postal service, you could well beat your letter back home?"

"I didn't want to change my mind. It was a way to help me stay the course."

"Historically Daisy, you have never had any trouble following through on what is important to you." He swallowed and continued to stare across the water. He had intended to ask another question of her this evening, but just now... the timing didn't seem right.

"Hugh..."

"Yes?"

"What you said... that made a difference to me... that time you likened this to the actual war. That made this horrifying random disease a tangible enemy to fight. Philip is right: the War Dad fought is not so far in the past that people don't remember what it is like to enlist in a fight against what threatens us. Dad said to me before he left that he had a responsibility to fight in a way that would make our world better for his family. Whether here... or there. He said Galloways were not people who stood on the sidelines. That is part of who I am, and I wanted to do the same... to fight with that same courage and commitment, in a way that would make my world better. When you said you were '*keeping the home fires burning*', the words to that song... even though I know it was a popular anthem for the Great War, it made the idea of not standing on the sidelines real for me. It also made me realise that I had to look after myself if I am to stay in active duty."

"Your Dad would be really proud of you. We all are. *I'm* so proud of you." He needed to say it again.

Daisy took a sip of the drink in her hand. "Hugh, you asked me once who I loved so deeply that it broke my heart. It wasn't any boyfriend... it was Dad. I can say that now. I was furious at him for insisting on going away to fight someone else's war. But by going... he made it his fight. He owned it. I was so angry about that, but then I realised he set that example because he wanted me to know there are things that I need to stand against too. Many people have acted like polio was someone else's problem, and they have not stood against it. That helped me understand why he was so determined to enlist when I begged him not to. When Violet got sick... that crack became a deep fissure, right down into the core of who I am. Going back to the hospital this time, after a while it was no longer penance... it became a way of contributing... a way to help others who were going through what we went through. Hugh, I know you have been praying me through this. I have felt God holding me and he has been healing those cracks in my heart."

He turned towards her. "The bricks that covered your heart then... are you telling me they are dismantled now?" His eyes had adjusted to the dark and he noticed the thoughtful furrow on her brow.

"Hmm... I thought about what you said. I wondered, what if my heart wasn't just bricked over, like you said... for protection. What if the pain had really turned my heart to stone: hard and impervious to feeling. I think to start with I did want to be a rock, a rock that can't be hurt. But then I realised a rock doesn't beat. It's not alive. It was Violet who inspired me to live. Really live. I got to the point where I wanted to be alive more than I needed to avoid the pain. I read something... something that meant a lot to me... in the Bible

God promises he will take away my heart of stone and transplant it with a heart of flesh. I think that knowing Violet had an undiagnosed heart condition... the idea that it could have been replaced with a healthy heart gave me something to think about. I've read about the research on this... and it is a way off still, but it is coming. I know it is. But in any case, even with all that happened, Violet still had a beating heart. She lived well, and truly, and full. Regardless of the stuff life threw at her, her heart was beating strong with hope."

"Yes, you are right about that... completely. There is not a better way to describe it." Hugh took a breath; there was still one more thing... "And the curse? What about that?"

"You were right. The curse is not me... but we live in a world that is writhing under a curse. I have stared that demon in the eyes, and I have had a hard time understanding why. If Jesus died on the cross to address the curse of death, then why do we still live with so much of it? The horrendous suffering of those kids' wards still haunts me. I have a nursing friend who told me she believes that right now, Jesus tackles it one person at a time, but there is a time coming when he addresses it for all eternity. I think because her brother had polio, I could hear what she said, more than anybody else. She got it... she understood what that kind of suffering meant. I saw how her belief in God gave her strength as she chose to still fight right in the middle of it all. She never wavered or withdrew to stand on the sidelines. And I realised this is exactly what Philip said... this is what we are all doing... fighting the good fight. So, with God's help, I will live well, fight well, nurse well... until His Kingdom comes. This is me, doing my bit to bring God's 'will on earth as it is in Heaven'. In Heaven I know there will be no Iron Lungs... no suffering like here. I know Violet is dancing up and down her own personal catwalk, having a marvellous time, modelling her stunning evening gown from her Australorp Collection. I believe that. This has given me hope."

"Oh, I like that picture! Just beautiful! Violet put her whole heart into everything."

"She did. And can I let you in on a secret? I think she actually knew my heart wasn't in any of your gestures of friendship. I thought I had made up such a clever cover-story, but I don't think she ever bought it. She knew me too well. Violet kept telling me I should give you a real chance. She said that more than once, even after we were going out on dates."

"Would you then... give me a chance Daisy? Can I stop being the hired help yet?"

She gasped. "It is a miracle that you are here Mr Marcum, given how severe I was on you. Yet right from the start, despite my accusations, you never behaved like the hired help."

"I believe I got my pay every week."

"Yes, but you did more than your allocated hours, and you cared more than a hireling." Daisy reached up and pulled out the pins from her hair that held her bun in place for the ceremony, and her hair fell softly over her shoulders. "I know I need to make an effort... to be gentler perhaps, like the way I was with Violet... I know I kept that very much compartmentalised."

He smiled. "I saw it often enough to know who you really are Daisy. Is it too soon to ask you to marry me?"

She gasped. "What? Are you serious?"

"Okay... well, I guess that is my answer."

"Well... I mean..."

"Daisy, I went along with your idea about pretending because I was frantic with worry for Violet. When you first brought the idea up, I thought it would be impossible to ever be serious about it. But at some point, impossible became possible... then it became necessary. Perhaps the storm was the turning point. I think working together like that, fighting for Violet's life, and seeing Lenwick rally, I think that anchored my hope... hope that we could face all sorts of storms like that together. Always."

"Always?"

"Yes. Will you marry me Daisy? One day? Would you consider that?"

"Sure. I think I will."

He sighed, relieved. "That is good news. Very good news."

Daisy was quiet and when he said nothing further, she laughed and reached for his hand. "Do you realise you just proposed to me, and I accepted? That means we are official now."

"I thought we have been official for a while."

"Yes... but now we are officially official. We are engaged." She laughed. "I like that. Never thought it would please me so."

He looked amazed at the smile on her face. "Official huh? Well then, since we are official it would be appropriate for me to give you this..." He reached into his pocket and pulled out a ring box.

He opened the lid and Daisy gasped. "Oh! I have no words. You... I..."

"Shh. Try it on." He slid it on her finger, enveloped by the dim shadows.

"Oh Hugh! This is incredible! A daisy!" She turned her hand and the daisy cluster on her finger glinted as the stones caught the dim light from the lamppost in the park. "It's beautiful! Are these real diamonds?"

"Very real. I have the receipt to prove it. I described to Violet what I wanted, and she drew it for me during one of Nancy's art sessions. I kept it and asked Mr Bollinger to find something like it. He is actually one of your greatest advocates. I think that is because he has made a lot of money out of me over the years. When he couldn't find anything, Mr Bollinger sent away the design and had it made up."

"Violet designed this? Oh, my giddy aunt...". She shook her head, speechless.

"That is yellow topaz in the centre. They call it Imperial Topaz. Think that is so they can charge more."

"It's beautiful... I don't know what to say."

"You don't have to say anything more. Your 'yes' is enough. Like I said, I have been hoping for a long time," he said with a grin, as he pressed his lips to her hand.

Daisy stood up, dragged Hugh to his feet and pulled him over to where the others were sitting. Jimmy had scrunched the greasy fish and chips newspaper into a ball, and they were using the cylinder from the confetti cannon as a bat to play cricket under the lamp light with Gus and Edith-Rose. Joe was wicketkeeper. Daisy interrupted their game to show everyone her 'Violet Original' ring. They huddled around, clambering for a look. Jimmy shrugged and threw the ball up in the air, annoyed that his winning innings had been disrupted. "Dunno what the big fuss is. We all knew this was comin'."

Philip came over and shook Hugh's hand. Daisy wrapped her arms around her big brother. "When you come home next, I want you to give me away. We are doing this."

"Oh, Daisy Hope... I... I won't be back for at least a year. I'm going to America. I've accepted an offer to join a research team sponsored by the National Foundation for Infantile Paralysis. It has a level of funding that means the work on refining vaccines is progressing ahead of other projects. Sorry, I didn't tell you before. I really didn't want to steal your thunder. Today is about you..."

Faith didn't wait to pour another round of drink into their tumblers and declared another toast. Philip was leaving to pursue his own dreams with that Galloway excellence.

Daisy wrapped her arms around her brother. "Congratulations! I know this is something that you have wanted for a while." She pushed back to look at him. "Is this you trying to get out of giving me away at my wedding?"

"Daisy Hope! Never. I'm honoured."

"A year it is then. You have to be here."

Faith grinned, as she picked up little David who started to whinge and rocked him gently on her shoulder. "I remember when you were a baby, Philip was so upset by the idea we might leave Bottlebrush Grove and have to give you back. Of all the babies Mum looked after... you were the one he wanted to keep."

"And now you want me to officially give you away. That doesn't seem fair Daisy Hope," Philip said with a grin.

"It is completely right though. You know it."

"Well then Daisy Hope, next Christmas we will have a wedding. Congratulations again to you both."

Sal came over and gave her daughter a hug. "Congratulations Darling. Your Dad would be so proud. And your Mother too... I've said it many times: you were her joy, just like her name. You have shown such courage through the most difficult storms. You are true to your name: Daisy Hope. And I am delighted that you will share your life with Hugh, to face together whatever storms may come."

Daisy enveloped her mother in a hug. "Oh Mum, we are anchored... I know that now... firm and secure... even when things crack through the core of who we are. That is our hope."

* * *

The end

Other books by this author

Matt's Boys of Wattle Creek

Maggie & Minotaur

Rose's Diary

Gems of Australia Series:
Sapphires of Hope
Rubies of Ambition
Emerald Dreams

Homes of Healing Series:
The Beachside Cottage
Petra Downs
The Writer's Retreat

Guthrie's Lot Series:
A Spacious Place
A Level Path
The Crying Tree

Pioneers of Grace Series:

Time of Grace

Circle of Grace

Journey of Grace

Mask of Grace

Crucible of Grace

Sculpture of Grace

Bottlebrush Grove Series

Shadows in the Corners

The Ragged Edges

Scratches across the Surface

Cracked through the Core

Children's Book

The Bush Olympics.